Poisoned Apple

By
Katherine McIntyre

Copyright © 2016 by Katherine McIntyre
ISBN: 978-1-68361-037-3
Cover art by Cora Graphics

Published by Decadent Publishing Company, LLC
Look for us online at:
www.decadentpublishing.com

A Note from the Author

Poisoned Apple holds a dear place in my heart, because I recreated it from the wreckage of one of my earliest manuscripts I wrote. My earliest works were my exploratory phase where I learned the basics, but trust me when I say, it wasn't salvageable. I stripped the story down to the barest elements and rewrote everything, from characters to the ending. I wanted Neve to be goth with a bitter attitude and cynicism that stemmed from her bad past. And I changed Brendan around completely, from a sweetheart, to someone damaged as well, because I didn't think Neve could relate to someone entirely good and whole considering how shattered she began and becomes through the story. The story that bloomed from that old manuscript became so intense for me and one I completely fell in love with. So, here's to hoping you enjoy reading Poisoned Apple as much as I enjoyed writing it and to other writers out there: writing is never a waste—the important themes and stories will always find a way to surface.

I can be reached at KMcIntyre@gmail.com. Feel free to contact me!

Dedication

To my friends and family for all their wonderful support and especially to my husband Rob who suffers through all the early drafts.

Chapter One

Neve knew this day would come. She'd been dreading it the past year, wondering what would happen and, for the life of her, unable to hazard a guess as to where the future would take her. After spending the past weeks worrying and hours in front of her computer screen talking to Internet strangers who had given her little useful advice, she'd grown wearier each day. At last, it had arrived—her eighteenth birthday.

Tugging at the spiked collar around her neck, she stole a glance at the front door of the house she'd grown up in. The peach siding created a gorgeous contrast to the stucco walls and the dark-brown roof tiles—a fairytale house in a fairytale suburban neighborhood. She rolled her eyes. Too bad life had been anything but.

She'd never wanted any of this, but such was life. Her dad hadn't asked when he'd ditched. No, he'd pranced out of the closet and ran off with his lover, leaving her with Veronica.

Her neck itched from too much sun. She'd been out here two hours, pacing around her cul-de-sac one hundred thirteen times since she'd returned from her shift at the café and, so far, had accomplished nothing. Her stomach clenched with the stark hollowness of what would happen the moment she walked through that door. Inside, Veronica would be waiting. As much as she hated confrontation and knew in her gut trouble was brewing, she'd have to deal with her stepmother at some point and was better off handling this mess without a bad case of sunburn. Neve let out a weary sigh then trekked up the paved walkway to her front door. *Time to face the beast.*

The moment she stepped inside, goose bumps prickled her skin from the blast of air conditioning. This place was too quiet. Even the usual sound of Veronica's soap, *Too Many Children*, was missing.

On a regular day, Neve would hide in her room with her earbuds in, Finnish death metal cranked to the highest volume to drown out the wooden acting and dramatic elevator music of Veronica's crap. The dense silence didn't bode well.

From a far corner of the house came a steady tap.

Not a drip of water or creak from worn floorboards. This was a purposeful sound as regular as a ticking clock. Neve eased toward the noise.

Based on the echo, it came from the study, one of the few places she used since her father's book collection still remained there. Veronica was one of those bright little flowers who "didn't read"—probably why Dad had chosen her in the first place all whopping two years and sixty-five days ago. The woman had been too dull to figure out he batted for the other team.

Swarovski vases glittered from the mantelpiece in the living room under the dusky rays of the afternoon sun. As she walked past, Neve clenched her jaw, tempted as always to dash them to the floor. Veronica wasted her money on flash—Gucci bags, Louboutin heels, whatever brand name, designer thing she could latch her manicured nails onto—leaving Neve to pay the bills. Shoving her hands into the pockets of her threadbare cargos, she hunched forward and headed for the study.

As she trod down the worn carpeting of her house, the tapping grew louder. *Her* childhood home. Yet, in the hellishly long year and seven days since her dad had left, her former home belonged to Veronica, from the new interior paint choices to the overblown elegant décor that came off cheesy in this suburban house.

Thirteen steps until I face Veronica.

She tightened her ponytail in an attempt to ready herself for the onslaught.

Five steps left.

Dipping into her purse, she slipped on all five of her rings, a variety of crosses and skulls.

Two steps.

The breath she'd been holding escaped as the situation settled into her bones.

Neve reached the landing. Squaring her shoulders, she marched straight down the hall to the first open doorway on her right. Most of the time, the study was one of her favorite places in the world. The huge windows let thick rays of sunlight pour onto the rosy hardwood, and dust caught the light like tiny fairies. A perfect place to read and escape. Today, however, black curtains covered the windows, casting the room into shadow. As she stepped inside, the mustiness of old books grew stifling, the air already thick with tension. Her father's old desk, one of those big mahogany monstrosities, was usually left unused since Neve preferred to curl up on the plush loveseat with a book rather than craning over a desk in some stiff-backed chair. Veronica sat in said chair, her toe tapping a percussive beat on the hardwood floor. Her sharp blue eyes were clear, her thin lips almost disappearing into a hard frown. Her stepmother's expression was familiar. Veronica ranged from miffed to raging on an everyday basis.

Blonde hair drawn into a no-nonsense bun, her new manicure the deep red of fresh blood, she'd even donned a blouse and slacks for the occasion, something Neve had forgotten Veronica owned. After Dad dodged out, Veronica had taken her job as a stay-at-home mom seriously—minus the mom part.

"Neve Wynn," Veronica said, her voice iced over. The tapping stopped.

"Veronica Wynn," Neve sassed before she could help herself.

"Renard. Veronica Renard." Her stepmother's eyes narrowed, two cold marbles glinting at her. "As of today, you're an adult."

A pregnant silence filled the room. *Not just an adult.* Since she'd turned eighteen, the child support from her father dried up—otherwise known as the sole reason Veronica hadn't kicked her to the curb yet.

Neve forced a bitter smile. "Oh, we're acknowledging my birthday this year?"

Veronica tapped her lurid fingernails on a piece of paper lying on the desk. "As we both know, you're going nowhere. No colleges applied for, no social life. The only job you've managed is your café job."

She took in a deep breath to control her temper. No colleges applied for because she didn't think she could make classes, not with working full time outside of school to pay the bills. No social life because no one liked hanging out with the damaged girl whose mom had died and whose father had ditched. If her own flesh and blood couldn't stick around, why would some schmucks from her hellhole of a high school?

"In essence, I've given you a roof over your head and taken care of you, even after your faggot father ran away," Veronica continued in the same haughty tone.

Her words stung, but the truth hurt worse—Neve's father had ditched the second he'd decided he no longer wanted a wife but a husband. If Mom had still been alive, maybe he wouldn't have left, but no one had noticed her heart problem—they hadn't paid close enough attention. Mom's death had destroyed her dad. She had blocked out all her memories of the funeral. Sometimes, she still woke up mornings having forgotten what happened—that her mom had died.

"God only knows what kind of a waste your mother was to raise a child like you. She must've killed herself from the shame."

Before she could stop herself, she lunged forward over the desk, her fist colliding with Veronica's jaw.

Blonde hair flew as her stepmother's head whipped to the side, a shriek ripping from her throat. Heat burned her cheeks with absolute hatred. Hatred for the woman who'd been dumped into her life with no care for her in the slightest. Hatred because Dad had left her with Veronica of all people. At her core, she always wondered, always questioned if the reason her mother had died and her father had run away had been because she was a terrible person. That her fate in life had always been to be saddled with this bitch of a stepmother.

Tears stung the corners of her eyes, but she wouldn't give Veronica the satisfaction of seeing her cry. Instead, Neve lifted her chin, throwing all of the fire she could muster into her glare. Veronica matched—her pointed nose up, her lips pinched as though she braved a wintry wind. Fire and ice, both for destruction would suffice.

Veronica's jaw reddened where she had clocked her, already the promise of a nasty bruise blossoming. "As I was saying," she continued in her dead, dispassionate voice, "as of today, you are no longer my problem. As of today, you are no longer welcome in this house. As of tomorrow, anything left in this house will be sold or tossed in the dump. Once the clock strikes midnight, you are to be out of here permanently."

The words hit her with a chill that prickled her skin. This was the fate she'd seen coming the second her dad had left. Yet she'd stayed, finishing out high school and working to keep Veronica from throwing her out on the street. All her efforts wasted. No mercy remained in the woman's gaze, not after Neve had lost her temper. Despite all the empty threats of turning her out on the streets in the past, this time was the real deal.

She swallowed, attempting to wet her bone-dry throat. The raging anger from before dissipated, infiltrated by the hollowness of abandonment, yet again.

Relatives were out of the question. Her father had been an only child, his parents long passed. Her mom's ultra-Christian family had disavowed him after they'd discovered he was gay. They'd tried to take Neve to Mass with them a couple of times, but once she started dyeing her hair black and wearing dog collars, any concern had vanished.

Veronica arched a brow, keeping her cool despite her discolored jaw. Silence descended upon the room again. She had nothing to counter with. No amount of pleading or arguing would dissuade the woman.

Time was running out. She must be out by midnight with anything she could carry. It took every ounce of effort she could muster, but Neve left the room. Even though her stepmother's gaze burned into her back and a breakdown lay three steps away, she held her chin high.

The second she stepped into the hallway, the darkened shadows seeped into her skin, sending a chill through her, even in the middle of summer. Her bedroom stood out like a blackened smudge at the end of the hall. She'd walked through the hallway a thousand times before, half-asleep or in the afternoon when returning from school. Hard to accept this would be one of the final times. How could she fit the fragments of her life into a single suitcase? Regardless, she'd have to try because, after tonight, she no longer had a home.

***

Neve stood in the middle of her bedroom, surrounded by dirty, rumpled clothes and stray books forming piles like tiny skyscrapers atop the carpet. Her eyes burned and her hands shook every time her mind drifted to the future. It took all her composure to rifle through the pieces of her life scattered across the floor.

All of the sudden, things she'd never given a second thought to mattered so much. The comfortable bed she'd slept in for as long as she could remember, the brass dresser lamp she and her mom had picked out at the thrift shop, even the stack of old paintings she'd saved from when she had time for art. All of those things meant more than she'd realized.

Her wide-open suitcase stared at her like a hungry beast, begging her to cram every last thing inside. Yet she couldn't. Trinkets and photographs from her past would be left behind. Other kids her age were going to college, packing for their dorm rooms, and figuring out the most important things to take. The difference was, their homes along with the rest of their stuff would be waiting for them at the end of the semester. *For me? This is good-bye.*

Into the suitcase went the green glass bead necklace Mom had given her. In went an extra pair of combat boots, bondage pants, cargos, and a couple tees still in decent shape. Last, in went *The Hobbit*, a copy Dad had given her which began her illustrious, well-defined relationship with books. She leaned against the bedpost, shoulders sagging as she heaved a sigh.

Weary didn't begin to cover it. Heartsick with fear might be a little closer, but the numbness infiltrated, seeping inside as her overwhelmed mind began to shut down. She slapped a pile of books which teetered over, sliding across the carpet. Downstairs, Veronica's high heels clicked on the hardwood—the worst noise in the world. No way Neve would give her the enjoyment of watching her walk out the door. She'd escape when the wicked stepmother exited the castle.

Pacing around her room, Neve found some other trinkets to toss into the suitcase, which was half her size. She weaved back and forth as she worked, the echoes of Veronica's stiletto clacks filling the house, as regular as a ticking clock. Maybe she'd catch the train into the city, see what waited for her there. She scrunched her nose. *Getting stabbed or shot at, that's what. City of Brotherly Love...biggest joke around.*

The neon numbers on her clock kept changing like the light outside her window. The sky faded from amber to magenta to the blue-black of night. Hour after hour ticked by. When at last, the front door slammed, Neve peered out her window. Veronica got into her Maserati. The second the engine revved, she forced herself to focus, throwing whatever remainders she could cram into the suitcase.

Time to exit. She struggled to lift the stuffed luggage. With an annoyed grunt, she dropped it to the floor, rolling it to the door. Before she left her room, she paused, twisting to peer over her shoulder. Books, clothes, knick-knacks scattered across every surface—her room resembled a bad yard sale. Still, she took a moment to absorb it all.

Carpe diem.

Tightening her grip on the luggage handle, she tugged her suitcase down the stairs, across the foyer, and out the door. Outside, the neighborhood was quiet, with no one aware of the trouble brewing in her life. As she'd walked along this street, a million stars stretched across an indigo canvas, holding all the freedom she'd yearned for every night. With literal independence forced upon her, all she wanted to do was curl up in her bed and sleep until all the misery went away.

Staring at the twinkling sky taunting her newfound lot in life, she raised her middle finger in the air.

"So much for karma. What a farce."

Chapter Two

After the awkwardness of traveling along the sidewalk at night through quiet neighborhood after quiet neighborhood, Neve was grateful to reach a busier part of town. Problem was, she still had no clue where to go. No friends she could try, at least none who'd give her a place to stay. She tightened her grip on the suitcase handle as she stepped underneath the streetlights, glad there weren't swarms of people to watch her walk of shame.

This close to Philly, the city sprawled over into her town, the gray buildings reaching higher and higher. She pulled her leather trench shut, not against the weather, since the occasional breezes did little to dispel the humidity on this still summer night, but because she walked the streets alone. Midnight black stained the sky like a spilled pot of ink, coating the chipped sidewalks all around her. Amidst the closed storefronts, distant cheers echoed from the couple of bars in her area.

With her baby face, no way Neve would get into any of those, ruling them out as loitering space. What could she even do? Find a park bench and squat until the cops arrested her? The green of the local park spread out in the distance, but after hearing the stories of what happened at night in Morris Park, she wasn't too keen on overnighting there.

Music blared from O'Malley's, the local Irish pub, and a couple guys scowled at her from the doorway. She returned the glare, not in the mood to deal with anyone's shit tonight. Hair-braiding salons and mystic shops littered the block, but she didn't need a psychic to predict her cards read "royally screwed."

After walking past a couple dozen blackened storefronts and an Applebees, she stumbled on a crack in the concrete. Her suitcase flew forward. When she stood, the white and yellow neon of a 24/7 diner assaulted her vision.

An old-timey sign, scrawled in a gothic font, announced The Cottage Diner. Visible through the large windowpanes, chestnut-and-cream booths lined the perimeter of the room. All the tables and the long sectional were made out of the same dark chestnut wood, giving the place a warm feel against the tan walls. At least she wouldn't have to worry about getting kicked out any time soon. Squaring her shoulders, Neve grabbed her suitcase and rolled it along the walkway toward the front door.

Once inside, the dueling scents of grease and bleach greeted her as well as a blast of cool air from the AC. Several dimming light bulbs along with a couple burnt-out ones had given the place an inviting but deceptive ambiance on the outside. When she stepped in front of the host stand, a woman with wide hunched shoulders grabbed a menu as she looked her over, her gaze pausing on the suitcase.

"Just one?" The lady's drawn-on eyebrows feigned concern.

"Yep, me." Ignoring the judgment, Neve followed her down the rows of booths.

The waitress stopped at one close to the far wall,

dropping the menu onto the table. "I'll be right back."

After cramming her suitcase on one side and slipping into the other, Neve tried to ignore the large table of people behind her filling the place with their chatter. Sitting alone in the booth wore on her worse than she could have imagined. It was one thing to feel the twist of loneliness, but, in this vacuum, she was devoid of a single familiar face. No one to turn to.

She pulled a small mirror out of her purse along with her eyeliner out to darken the lines around her gray eyes. Long ago she'd come to terms with her porcelain-doll-meets-vampire appearance. Besides, if fate had sentenced her to a solitary existence, why not give people a reason to avoid?

"She threw away my Batman comics," a guy's voice came from the large table behind her. "Tossed them out with no concern for the fact they were worth some decent money."

The waitress reappeared, tapping a pen on the pad she held. "What can I get for you?"

Prickles of cold from the air conditioning seeped in past Neve's coat, causing her to shiver. "Coffee, I guess."

The woman nodded and disappeared through a door that led to the kitchen.

"Thank everything holy you guys broke up. You can do much better than Stacy," another guy chimed in from the noisy table.

"Right? You can have your pick of the place. Like what about this one?" another voice asked, way closer than the others. "Hey, you."

Neve frowned. The voice came from above her. A face peered overtop the booth separator.

She tilted her head to the side. "You mean me?"

"Yeah, are you waiting for someone?" He had tanned skin and shaggy brown hair that drifted in front of his eyes like an Old English Sheepdog.

"Uh." Her words stuck in her throat as she stared down at the table. Screw it. Talking to anyone at this point was better than sitting on her own. "No, I'm not waiting for anyone."

"You're by yourself? Come sit with us." He gave her a wide grin, one of those infectious ones that made her want to smile with him.

She bit her lip, staring out the window. These people didn't need to know her whole deal, so maybe for once she could be someone other than the damaged girl.

"Thanks." She offered a half smile and grabbed her suitcase.

The guys made space for her on the edge, so she slid in, trying to drop her baggage on the ground without drawing notice. Within seconds of her sitting down, four guys glanced from her to the monstrosity beside her.

"Why the suitcase?" the puppy-ish guy asked, those brown eyes warm with curiosity.

"I'm moving." She tried vagueness, hoping they wouldn't pry much. Of course too much to hope for— she could spot the questions coming the second he opened his mouth again.

"Moving where? One suitcase looks more like a hotel stay or something. Are you a gypsy?" His grin widened with his excitement.

She fought to hold back the eye roll. "Yep, that's me. Vagabond extraordinaire. I've got a suitcase full of rat bones and tea."

"Please, ignore Gabe," one of his friends interjected. "He's got the sensitivity of a caveman."

This guy looked a couple years older with sharp black eyebrows and a trimmed beard. Based on his pressed dress shirt and nice black slacks, chances were, he'd come from work. He stuck his hand out. "I'm Martin. Nice to meet you."

She shook his hand, glancing over to the other two guys at the table, both of whom couldn't be more than a couple years older than her. One of the guys wore a green hoodie, his sharp cheekbones and square jaw defined by shadows. He had the kind of blue eyes that saw straight through your bullshit, but at the moment, his type was too intense to handle. The other guy was so scrawny his flannel shirt hung loose along his shoulders, the sleeves dangling past his wrists. When he blinked, his long eyelashes fluttered against his glasses.

"Well, what if it's a suitcase full of dead body parts?" Gabe argued, ignoring the dirty look Martin shot him. "I feel we deserve to know if you're on the run or something."

"He makes a valid point," Glasses spoke up. "We don't want some mobster problems brought down."

The other guy kept quiet, still watching her.

Neve let out a sigh, frustrated. As much as she wanted to ignore her damage and leave it behind like her suitcase, her baggage followed her wherever she went. "Not a mobster or a gypsy or on the run. Nothing glamorous. Got kicked out, that's all." As she admitted the truth, her cheeks flushed with shame.

"So a hobo, is it?" Gabe tapped his spoon on the table to a staccato beat.

"Quit being a jerk." Martin elbowed him in the side.

"Sorry to hear." Frowning, Glasses gave her a nod. "I'm Colin, by the way. Happen to have a name, or is it random goth girl?"

"Neve Wynn. Less random. More homeless goth girl."

The waitress approached with a cup of coffee but blinked on reaching the empty booth.

Neve raised her hand. "Over here."

The waitress pursed her thin lips. "You're with this bunch now? Watch out, they're nothing but trouble."

Colin grinned. "Not fair, Jennie. You know you love us."

"Right, because I love you squatters. This isn't a

homeless shelter, you know." A hint of a smile tugged her lips as she walked away.

"She wasn't referring to you, Neve." Gabe sipped his Mountain Dew. "So you know."

She snorted. "I figured as much. Just because I got kicked out doesn't mean I'm some delicate daisy. I'm not going to wilt at the slightest breeze blowing my way."

"Let me guess," the guy from the corner drawled, his intense gaze swinging her way. "After getting in a fight with Daddy, you're on the prowl for another guy to mooch off of."

"Seriously, Brendan?" Colin shot him a glare. "Can you be a little more bitter?"

Her cheeks heated again as she clenched the sides of the table. *Screw him.* She sucked in a deep breath as venom flooded through her system. "You caught me. Looks like you've got me pegged, figuring out my master plan and all."

"What?" Brendan straightened. "Tell me I'm wrong."

She clenched her jaw. Sitting with this group of jerks had been a terrible idea. Because, like she'd seen over and over, no one wanted a damaged girl.

"She doesn't have to justify herself." Martin crossed his arms. "Just because Stace was a bitch doesn't mean all women are. We invited her over here, and you're being an ass."

"Oh no, I'm sure he's read me quite right." Reaching down, she grabbed the handle of her suitcase. It took every ounce of resolve not to fall apart. This day had been hell, and the short reprieve had ended up being another miserable trap. "I'm homeless for shits and giggles, not because child support ran out today and my bitch of a stepmother'd had enough of the familial farce. Thanks for reminding me my baggage isn't your problem."

Brendan's shoulders sagged, and he wouldn't meet her eyes. "I'm going for a smoke."

Neve stood, almost crashing into him as he dodged past her in his beeline to the door. Time to return to her booth and see if she could get a different seat as far away as possible from them. If not, it'd be out the door to find a new diner. Next time, she wouldn't be gullible.

A hand grabbed her shoulder. She glanced back to

see Gabe.

"Hey, I'm sorry for what he said." His eyebrows scrunched together, concern written all over his face.

"Don't listen to him," Martin agreed. "Please stay. I promise we'll keep his rudeness under wraps."

As her throat tightened, Neve didn't trust the breath she held. Truth was, she didn't want to leave. For a couple hours, she wanted to pretend she wasn't on her own in the world even if it meant checking her pride. Gabe squeezed her shoulder, and she sighed.

She sat down, her hand still curled around the handle of her suitcase, ready at any moment to bolt. She'd let her guard down, foolish her, but she wouldn't again.

"Did your stepmom really kick you out because the child support dried up? She must be wicked harsh." Gabe shook his head. Most folks she would've told to screw off, but something about Gabe's innocent demeanor calmed her down.

"Don't be rude. Maybe she doesn't want to talk about that crap." Martin swatted at his shoulder.

She shrugged, cupping her mug of coffee and letting the warmth seep in through her fingertips.

"It's a legit question. Yeah, we didn't get along well."

"Dad's not in the picture?" The way Colin studied her, he seemed to piece things together while they talked.

"Bingo." She took a deep drink of coffee, wishing it was whisky.

"I assume Mom's not here either, or else you'd be going there." Colin's mouth twisted with a frown. "Brendan wasn't even close to the mark. You've got a shit situation on your hands."

"Hence the dilemma. How long do you think they'll let me camp here before kicking me out?" She tried to deliver with a grin, but her smile faltered at the worry of where to go when she had to leave.

"Through the night, milady." Martin winked. "We've pulled a couple all-nighters in our day. I think we can muster another one. Or at least some of us can. I'll have to duck out since I've got work in the morning."

"Grad students don't sleep. I'll wait with you." Colin adjusted his glasses on his nose.

A familiar man wearing a green hoodie stalked in through the glass doors, heading their way. Neve tensed, ready for an argument. This time she wouldn't get caught off guard, wouldn't let herself get hurt. Brendan stopped in front of her, hands in his pockets, lips pursed as he hesitated, those turbulent ocean-blue eyes catching hers. Lifting her chin a little higher, she kept his gaze.

To her surprise, he tugged his hand free from his pocket, holding it out in front of her. "Hi, my name's Brendan. Apparently, when I go through breakups, I turn into an insensitive prick. Can we start over?"

She stared at him hard, not sure what caused the turnaround. Even though she didn't trust him for anything, he was a friend of these guys, so she'd play nice. After all, they'd agreed to stay with her, a complete stranger.

Gripping his hand, she shook. "The name's Neve, not damsel in distress."

A ghost of a smile flitted to his lips as he slid into the booth.

"You in for a late night, Brendan?" Colin threw a pen at his head, but Brendan caught it midair. "Since this chica has no family and no place to go, we figured we'd stay so she didn't have to wander the streets alone tonight."

"How taxing," Brendan said dryly, "doing what we already do most nights. It'll take so much effort."

"Speak for yourselves. I work a respectable job." Martin leaned back in the booth, his arms resting on the ledge.

"Investment banking is not respectable. You've got a shark's career." Brendan speared several french fries with his fork.

"Agreed." Gabe rolled his straw wrapper into tiny balls. "I'll keep my gig at the Rusty Nail."

"Name like that? Great resume fodder. Your boss is a Scandinavian nut job," Colin piped in.

Neve settled into her seat, comfortable listening to them sling insults between themselves with the ease of longtime friendships. Nothing like the tense encounters she'd grown used to.

Chapter Three

Minutes flipped to hours in what seemed like seconds. Neve checked her phone every once in a while, but the best clock was the gradual brightening of the sky.

Martin checked out first, leaving around two in the morning. Colin followed suit around four since he still had classes the next day. Which left her, Brendan, and Gabe.

She'd thumbed the handle of her suitcase until her fingertip turned raw. The waitress had left once her shift ended. Another woman swung by to check on them, but the coffee refills came less frequent, making the fight to stay awake harder. Yet even when a new morning hit, she still wouldn't have anywhere to rest her head. Conversation dragged to occasional mumbles rather than the steady stream of snark from earlier in the night.

She knew what came next though, every time Gabe glanced at the clock or Brendan checked his phone. The moment the first streaks of dawn crawled across the sky, her time was up.

Gabe rubbed his eyes then pulled on his hoodie. "I'm sorry, Nevie, it was nice meeting you. I hope we see you again—"

"Yeah, yeah. It's time to go." She strained to smile.

He saluted and strolled toward the door. While their company had made the night more bearable, the morning destroyed any shred of escapism remaining. This was the real deal—she had nowhere to go but a homeless shelter or the streets.

Before Brendan could give her a good-bye, too, she rose, tugging her suitcase with her. "Thanks for waiting with me. I mean it."

The walk to the front door stretched out like an endless corridor. Not only did her vision cloud from exhaustion, but fear of the unknown cluttered her sleep-deprived mind. She walked out the chrome doors, leaving behind the safe haven she'd found for the night.

Morning transformed her town with lavender streaks, casting everything in a cold, tranquil light. The sidewalks were barren, and the trills of the early birds echoed throughout the dew-laden air. Before she could stroll down the walkway, a hand tugged on her arm.

"Neve, wait up," Brendan said from behind her.

She gave him a half smile. "I'm not traveling too fast, don't worry."

"The guys are going to give me shit for being a sucker again, but I feel bad about being an ass back there. If you need a couch to crash on, I have one. Call this lack of sleep delirium. Even though I have a bad track record with mooches taking advantage, I'm going to give you a shot."

She blinked, not quite registering his words. She pressed her tongue to the roof of her mouth as her sense of survival warred with the immense pride that got her into trouble. The same guy who'd given her shit for being a user was giving her the opportunity to prove him right.

"Stacy taught me one thing, though...not to get

suckered again. If you pull the same type of shit, I'll cast you out. No remorse." His mouth softened for a moment then formed a hard line again. In the morning light, a flush crept onto his cheeks, highlighting his strong cheekbones.

She swallowed, hard. Pride could take a hike. She needed a lease on time. A couple days to find a place to live. If she turned his offer down, she'd be forced to wander the streets. He watched her with those carved eyebrows knitted together as he waited for a response.

"Thank you," she whispered. Her eyes stung, tears threatening to break free.

"Yeah, no problem." He ran a hand through his short chestnut hair, glancing down at the sidewalk. "Well, I guess follow me, then."

A sniff escaped her, and she grabbed at her nose, trying to force down the emotions threatening to pour out. "Damn allergies," she grumbled, hoping he didn't notice the scratchiness. She caught the hint of a smile on his lips, but, seconds later, it vanished, claimed by seriousness again.

"Lead on, sir." Neve inhaled a shaky deep breath

before following him as they set off toward his apartment.

Chapter Four

Following a stranger home wasn't one of Neve's brightest ideas, but given her current state of affairs, it happened to be her best option. Despite accepting his offer, she still wasn't sure what to make of Brendan. He had the muscles and swagger of a jock, the kind of guy she'd avoided in high school—at least when she used to associate with people. Based on his apology earlier, he couldn't be all jerk. But at this stage of the game, her fuzzy mind mixed left and right as though she'd never learned the difference.

The early morning hours were too hushed for idle chatter, so they walked down the sidewalk in silence. A mere five minutes later, they arrived in front of a once-white, four-story apartment building. The metal-rimmed sign read New Haven Apartments.

She followed him up to the third floor. The jangle of his keys echoed through the corridor, the sound bouncing from one end to the other. Her feet scuffed over the worn patches in the carpeting as she scanned the walls, cracked and exposing crumbled plaster in sections.

"Here it is," he mumbled, jamming his key into the dead-bolt lock for apartment B-07.

The slight filter of gray morning light slipped through the slatted blinds. He flicked on the lamp, casting the room in a pinkish-yellow glow. Piles of books and magazines lay on and around the coffee table with a piece of duct tape hanging off one of the legs. A blanket lay piled on the side of a faded brownish couch that must've once been maroon. She didn't give a fig if it was stained, though—compared to sleeping on a bench outside, these were five-star accommodations.

She dropped her suitcase next to the couch before taking a seat. Exhaustion flooded her in one crashing wave while, at the same time, relief trickled down her spine. Brendan ducked into his room, and thumps came from behind the door. Seconds later, he emerged holding a blanket and a pillow—more than she'd expected.

"I can't thank you enough." She accepted his offerings, the intensity of her gratitude causing her to suck in a deep breath. Perhaps she'd done herself a wrong by assuming everyone would treat her like crap. Already on her first day out of Veronica's clutches, she'd witnessed a better side of humanity.

"Don't thank me." He scratched the back of his neck and glanced her way. "Get your shit together so you can get out of here, or else, in a week, I'll have to kick you out myself."

There he went, ruining the moment. She pressed her tongue against her teeth to keep from the smart retort on her lips. He had offered a place to stay, so she shouldn't expect anything more. Like basic courtesy or politeness.

"Don't worry. I don't plan on making homelessness my career." She sank into the couch and tugged the blanket over her, even though his apartment was already so warm it verged on sticky.

"Good night, homeless girl." He waved a hand in

the air before sauntering off to his bedroom.

"Good night, Prince Smartass," she mumbled.

"What was that?" He turned around, leaning against the doorframe.

"I said I'm glad I'm not sleeping on grass."

He snorted then walked into his bedroom, slamming the door behind him.

She pulled the blanket to her nose. The contradictions between his actions and words confused the hell out of her.

Dawn's harsh light seeped through the blinds, deepening the crevices in the floorboards while widening every chip on each chair surrounding the big oak table in his open kitchen. With her mind turned to sludge from stress and lack of sleep, any plans she made would be half-assed at best. Instead, she needed to catch some shut-eye while she could. She pulled the blanket overtop her head, eyes aching as she squeezed them shut.

***

Neve woke to the taste of cotton in her mouth and

a woolen blanket over her head. She thrashed, the blanket sticking to her sweat-slicked arms. The musty scent of cinnamon tickled her nose.

She froze. This wasn't her bed. These surroundings....

She let out a sigh, remembering where she was. The night before, Brendan had taken her in, even giving her a couch to crash on. Today began the apartment hunt. Hell, today began day one of her independence.

Tossing the blanket off, she strolled around the apartment. The door to his room lay open, and a static silence consumed the house, interrupted by the occasional rush of cars or honks from outside. On the oaken table in his kitchen lay a note.

Left for work. Keep the door unlocked when you leave. I'll be back at six.
Brendan

A sigh of relief coursed through her at not having to deal with Sir Grouch-A-Lot. She stepped into the bathroom and splashed some water on her face, trying to rid herself of the greasy staleness.

Her hair, midnight black and thick as a skein of yarn, hung down her shoulders in a tangled mess. She finger-combed the strands before tugging the length into a ponytail. Her dark eyeliner had smudged overnight, creating raccoon circles around her eyes. After cleaning the mess off, she tossed on black leggings and a longer black tunic. Grabbing her liquid liner, she lined her lids with two streaks like war paint. After all, this was a battle of survival for finding a roof over her head. She would succeed, too—if only to give her father and Veronica a big middle finger when she made it on her own.

Today, she was off work, so she had an entire day to figure out where to live. Waitress wages in the suburbs would be tough, but tough she could handle. A balmy breeze cut through the summer humidity as she stepped out the door.

Something about the sunlight, about walking free from the sodden misery of her old life with Veronica, brought a spring to her step. Even if she got lonely in a place by herself, solitude trumped paying the bills for a bitch who didn't care about her. For the first time in her life, she strode through the familiar streets with a new sense of purpose—freedom.

She tightened the laces on her combat boots before heading toward the library. Books, Internet access, and a free place to spend her day. It'd give her a chance to scan through apartment listings on Craigslist. Brendan wouldn't have to tolerate her for too long because, once she put her mind to it, she'd find something.

***

After hours of switching between jotting down apartment listings and escaping into the latest Jim Butcher novel, Neve was surprised to find most of the day had already passed. She checked out the book and left because she had a stop to make before heading over to Brendan's.

Upon returning to the apartment, the lazy afternoon sun had deepened. Shadows coated his entire place. She stumbled over one of his magazine piles then tripped her way to the couch. From there at least she could locate the light.

Once situated, she set to work. The kitchen wasn't much larger than the other small rooms in his apartment, but it served her purposes. After spreading ingredients along the mottled slate countertops, she got to work, setting pasta to a boil and chopping vegetables for the primavera. While living with Veronica, if she didn't cook, she didn't eat, so she'd learned how to make the basics.

Soon, the scent of butter, garlic, and sautéing vegetables overtook the apartment, cutting through the mustiness. Neve dug through an odd assortment of pots and pans, all in disrepair, but she could make do. At almost six on the dot, the door creaked, and Brendan strolled in.

"You made dinner?" His eyes were unreadable, same as the tone in his voice, all of which made her nervous. What if she'd overstepped her bounds? Would he boot her out? Preparing dinner had seemed like a nice idea, but making it for a complete stranger? What had she expected to come from the gesture?

"Sorry." She threw her hands up in defense. "Figured I'd at least start putting a dent into how much I owe you for giving me a temporary place to sleep." She'd emphasized *temporary*, and, by the hint of a smirk on his lips, he'd understood.

"Don't apologize. I haven't had someone cook a meal for me in ages. I was surprised, that's all." He sauntered into the kitchen, wearing a white shirt and black pants. Before taking a seat, he draped a grimy jacket on the back of the chair. "Being a cook saps your will to prep food when you get home. Especially when it's a one-person dinner."

"Well then, enjoy." She carried two laden plates to the table. The pasta primavera cast curls of steam into the air, and the vegetables—from the purplish red onions to the diced yellow peppers—created a rainbow on the plate. Alongside, she'd included some homemade garlic bread, dripping with butter.

He speared his fork into the meal without hesitation. The vegetables scattered around his plate as he tore into the food. She picked at her dinner, savoring each bite, grateful she'd even had a place to cook tonight.

"Where do you work?" he asked between bites. His gaze darkened. "Or are you one of those girls who can't keep a job and are looking for a—" He caught himself with a deep breath. There he went, ruining any chance at decent conversation again.

"Comparing me to your ex?" She lifted a brow, keeping her boiling temper under rein. "I do, in fact, have a job. I've worked at the café up the road since I was sixteen."

Focusing on the table, he chased a piece of broccoli around his plate. "Opened my mouth too soon again. So, Neve-with-a-job Wynn, why didn't you move out on your own, then? Why deal with the stepmother?"

"I'm eighteen, genius. Literally turned it yesterday. You try getting an apartment any younger and see how that goes for you."

He choked on his pasta. "Wait, you're eighteen? I thought you were my age."

"Which is?" She guessed over twenty-one based on the six-pack she'd seen in the fridge.

"Twenty-two. Way too old to be taking in homeless high schoolers."

And back to jackass. Any argument over her age would make her seem childish, so she didn't bother.

He carried their empty plates to the sink. "Well, thank you for the meal. It was a refreshing change of pace."

Despite his attitude, his defined chin and long lashes marked him as gorgeous, and he knew it. With the sleeves of his stained white shirt rolled, his defined biceps and thick forearms were on display. A snake wove its way down his arm, a compliment to the tattoo artist because, unlike a lot of the hokey flash she'd seen, the detail in the piece stood out.

As he passed her on his way to his bedroom, those intense blue eyes of his darted her way, reminding her she was gawking. "I'm heading to the diner again if you'd like to join."

"Two nights in a row? What an exciting life you lead." Not giving him a chance to retort, she said, "I would like to join, though."

He smirked before shutting the door behind him.

Neve glanced down to her phone. No word from Veronica. Maybe she'd gotten lucky and her stepmother hadn't followed through on throwing out her stuff. She'd have to investigate after her shift tomorrow, though. Her gig at the Cozy Corner café was the one thing that hadn't failed or abandoned her.

Leaning back on the couch, she lifted her foot since one of the strings on her boot had loosened. Too lazy to hunch over, she pulled her knee to her chest to tie the laces.

The bedroom door swung open, and Brendan walked out. His gaze lingered as he scanned her from head to toe again. Realizing her shirt had hiked up, exposing more skin than intended, she sprung to her feet, like a cat pretending it hadn't run into a wall headfirst. A flush heated her cheeks.

He'd changed into gray cargos, a white wife-beater, and a blue-and-green tartan overshirt. Of course he managed to look good with minimal effort.

"You took so long I got bored." She widened her smile, teeth showing. "Next time freshen up quicker, princess."

He snorted, pocketed his wallet, and grabbed his keys from the hook on the wall. "If that's what happens when you're left alone for five minutes, I'm terrified to fathom what you did all day."

Chapter Five

Same as the night before, their group took over the back table, visible through the wide windows, even from where she stood in the parking lot. Neve spotted Gabe and Martin again, but instead of Colin, two other guys waited inside. She walked to the door, ready to stroll in, but Brendan stopped and pulled out a cigarette. She paused, not sure she wanted to head in without him.

"Don't tell me you're nervous." He arched an eyebrow as a steady stream of smoke escaped his lips. That man somehow managed to say the exact words to get under her skin.

"Not in the slightest." She clenched her jaw before she marched inside.

Gabe spotted her at once and waved both hands

for all the world like an excited puppy. "You're alive! You didn't get stabbed and left for dead on the streets."

Martin nodded her way, and the other two guys gave polite waves.

"How did you know we were going to be here?" Gabe gestured for her to sit. "Or were you returning in hopes of finding us again? I bet it's that."

She blinked several times as she slipped into the booth. He was an onslaught of hyper.

"Neve, this is Conor." Martin jerked a thumb at the guy wearing the tan trench and whose long black hair curled around his ears. His arched nose protruded, same as his chin, giving him features straight off of a statue. "And this is Ian." A slimmer guy with pierced labret, ears, and eyebrows stared her way. The chains on his shirt clinked as he adjusted his glasses.

"Great to meet you guys, but is this a boys' club or what? I've only met men around you folks." She arched an eyebrow at Martin.

He let out a belly laugh. His collared shirt was undone a few buttons, and his dark hair lay in messy strands rather than the slicked look from the day before. "Seems most girls avoid us like the plague. A bachelors' club, maybe?"

"Don't let him deceive you," Ian spoke up. "My girl Jess comes out every once in a while, but she works a weird shift."

"Oh, thank God, I was beginning to worry what I'd stumbled onto." She gave him a grin. "Speaking of couples, how long have you two been together?" She gave a pointed glance to Martin and Gabe.

"Ha, if I swung that way, I'd pull better than this ruffian." Martin leaned over to scruff Gabe's mop of a head.

"They both wish I was interested, but I prefer my guys young and dumb." Conor shrugged, tucking a curl behind his ear. His eyes twinkled with a devilish glint.

Brendan came inside, threading the air with the scent of tobacco. "Make some space, people." He nudged into the spot next to her.

"What did you do today, Neve?" Martin asked. "Don't tell me you slept on a park bench, or I'll feel like a jerk."

She snuck a glance at Brendan, but he wasn't looking her way. Fine, if he wanted to play the avoidance game, she could create a cover story.

"She stayed at his place." Ian pointed a finger their way.

A blush hit her cheeks full force as she opened her mouth. "I—"

"Seriously, Ian?" Brendan quipped. "How did you figure it out?"

"She's a poker player's wet dream. Sorry, sweetheart, you can't bluff for anything." Ian shrugged, one of his crooked teeth poking out with his smile.

Neve balled her hands into fists underneath the table, resting them on her thighs. "Nah, you're right. When you're as pale as I am, it's pretty tough."

"Honesty's no crime." Ian swung his honey gaze to Brendan. "What I'd like to know is why he tried to hide it."

"Because it's no big deal, and you assholes would turn it into one." He flagged down Jennie for coffee. Neve piped in for some before the waitress could run away.

Every eye focused their way, for the most part on Brendan. She inched nearer to Gabe.

"After the way you ripped on her last night, you owed her a place to stay." Martin shrugged. "I won't give you crap."

"Yeah, I couldn't care less." Gabe focused on launching a paper ball across the room using his fork.

Ian was busy giving Brendan eye signals, which Neve couldn't come close to interpreting. Ladies weren't the only ones with the weird eye communication ritual, but regardless of gender, she'd never been subtle enough to comprehend.

"Fine. Well, I'm giving her a temporary couch to crash on until she finds a place. Or until a week's up, whichever comes first." He glared Ian's way.

"If he has the audacity to kick you out, let me know, and you can crash on my couch," Martin offered.

She scratched the nape of her neck, embarrassed by their generosity. "If I don't have a place soon, I'm going to oust myself. I couldn't stand being that indebted to anyone."

Jennie returned with their coffees, plinking them

down onto the table. Neve grabbed for hers, ignoring the light scorch of heat against her palms.

"Well, since we've embarrassed the poor girl, let's take some of the heat off her. Who wants to hear about the guy I met at the Swiss Barn Door the other week?" Conor banged a fist on the table, which caused the cups and silverware to jangle.

"Yeah, I think I'll pass." Martin frowned, grabbing a fry from his plate.

"Did you take him home and treat him right?" A goofy grin filled Gabe's face.

"Well, the poor boy *wanted* me to mistreat him." Conor's eyes glinted with his devilish smile.

Brendan, Ian, and Martin all groaned at once. As Neve laughed, Conor launched into detail about his latest exploit. She settled into the booth, the combination of heat from the lamp and the scorching coffee warming her chest. Maybe at last she was heading in the right direction.

***

Under the early morning sun, Neve jogged down

the sidewalk. On Thursdays, Veronica left the house for spin class which gave her a short window of time to get in and out of the house without being noticed. The broad sunlight beat down on her back, sinking into the fibers of her dark-gray button-down. Morning wasn't the best time of day for sneaking, but most folks in the neighborhood had seen her growing up there and wouldn't count it as breaking in.

She passed the strip malls along the sidewalks she'd trod with her suitcase the other night. Several blocks later, a familiar street sign rose into view. The closer she got to her street, the louder her heart thumped. She curled her fingers around her purse straps, and a sweat broke out on the nape of her neck. Being here flooded her with memories, ones she'd rather leave buried in the past.

The dark-brown roof tiles came into sight first, then the pearly white stucco exterior. No car in the driveway meant the evil stepmother had followed routine. She banked on the chance Veronica hadn't changed the locks. This whole venture was a crapshoot anyway, but Neve would kick herself if she didn't at least try.

As she approached the front door, she remembered doing the exact same thing the other day, and her throat dried. The summer sun pulsed down in streams, promising a heat wave with every last ray. She tested the doorknob. Locked but she'd expected as much, so she tried her key.

To her relief, it clicked, and she swung the door open.

Those sickening Swarovski vases sparkled in the sun, greeting her as she walked into the foyer—one of the many things she wouldn't miss about her former home. Not like it'd been much of a home since Veronica moved in. No time to waste checking through the house even though most of the furniture and possessions belonged to her family.

She ascended the steps, sweat beading along her forehead. Being in this house had left an oppressive mark on her she'd never even realized. At the end of the corridor, her door loomed, one she wasn't sure she wanted to open. Would her things be there, or had Veronica followed through with her threats?

She opened the door.

Her stomach dropped. *Empty.*

Crumpled papers, crumbs, dirt, and a pen wedged in the corner all littered the floor. Her bed and the dresser still remained, including the lamps. Everything else was gone. Her piles of books, her porcelain cats perched on the dresser, and the clothing that had scattered the floor all had vanished. Photographs were missing, as though her entire past had vanished. Veronica must have hauled everything off to the trash the second Neve had left. Her breath left her in one sharp exhale as she sank to the floor.

They were just things. Things could be replaced, and at least she wasn't on the streets. But no matter how she reminded herself, this act drove the knife in, reminding her this current predicament wasn't temporary. Veronica had kicked her out, and she could never go home.

Her blood boiled. Screw that harpy of a woman with her bleached blonde hair, those ice chips for eyes, and her iron heart nothing penetrated. She rose off the floor, clenching her fists. God, she needed something to smash.

She stormed to the bottom of the stairs where she faced all five of the Swarovski vases. They sparkled in the sun like diamonds, small vessels of pure money. Her fingers curled around the long fluted neck of the first one.

This is for all the times Veronica ignored me, pretending I didn't exist. She hurled the vase at the wall. It splintered into a thousand pieces like a splash of water glittering through the air. Her breath hitched as the shards flew.

For the past two birthdays I spent working to avoid the emptiness at home. She smashed the next one.

For those nasty jabs Veronica liked to slip in about my weight. For saying I'm plain, ugly. That I'll never find someone who could love me. Her jaw clenched as she lobbed the next two vases, one after another hitting the wall in tiny explosions.

For saying Mom didn't care. That Dad was worthless. For telling me I'd never amount to shit. Because despite how much her father's betrayal had scarred her and how her mother's death still haunted her morning and night, she had survived and would continue to fight. Yeah, she was flawed. Damaged goods.

Her fingers tightened around the throat of the last vase so hard it exploded in her grip. Shards flew everywhere, slicing her hands, her forearm, and cascading to the floor like snow glistening on a winter morning. *The name Neve Wynn will be an insult no more.*

She marched out the door. The sidewalk seemed a little sunnier as she headed toward the apartment. Even though she hadn't managed to score the rest of her stuff, satisfaction thrummed through her veins after smashing Veronica's vases. That was a memory for the books.

Her palms were sliced, a couple shards still embedded in them. When she got to the apartment, she'd have to douse the mess with some alcohol. Last thing she needed would be to waitress with jacked-up hands.

After about a ten-minute walk, passing The Cottage Diner and all, Brendan's apartment complex came into view. She ascended the stairs to his apartment complex, a bounce to her step she hadn't felt in years. At the end of the corridor, she stopped in front of his apartment, opened the door, and stopped.

A girl sat on the couch, petite with wavy beach hair and eyes the color of a summer sky. Her lips downturned with her pout as soon as her baby blues flashed Neve's way.

"Who the hell are you?"

Chapter Six

"My name's Neve." She thrust her hand out but, realizing blood smeared her palm, retracted it fast. "Hold on, give me a second."

She rushed to the sink, dunking her hands under a stream of lukewarm water. Pink filled the basin until the shallow cuts stopped bleeding and the shards had washed out. The woman from the other room entered the kitchen. Her eyebrows knitted together, and irritation rolled off her in waves, coating the air with tension.

"This is Brendan's apartment, yeah?" She crossed her arms over her chest.

Neve bit her lip. Hooray for awkwardness. "Yeah, this is."

Wrong answer. The annoyance on her face darkened to rage, causing the room to heat a couple dozen degrees. Neve focused on her palms, scanning them for any remaining shards of glass.

"When's he getting back?" the blonde spat, the venom in her voice reminiscent of Veronica.

Neve shrugged. "Beats me."

She had her guesses who the girl might be, based on Brendan's raging anger toward females. Plus, blondie lounged in his apartment like it was no big deal. However, as a couch crasher here, she needed to keep out of his business. Already she'd pissed off said stranger.

Rather than bothering to start a conversation, Neve sunk onto the couch and pulled her library book from her purse. This chick was hunting for a fight, and if she engaged, it'd cause more hell for Brendan. Despite the shit way he handled most conversations, his actions had proved him a good guy. She owed him for giving her a place to crash.

Neve buried her face in her book while the unwelcome houseguest paced the kitchen. If she'd known Brendan's number, she would've texted him a warning, but instead, he was in for a tense, cranky surprise when he came home.

Pace, pace, pace.

She twitched, glancing up from her book. The girl paused to shoot her a dirty glare. Neve let out a sigh, continuing to read. After a while of not getting any attention, the mystery girl took a seat in the kitchen and amused herself by scanning through her phone. Not her problem. The book was just getting good when the door opened with a creak.

"Hey, don't tell me you sat here all day," Brendan said, hands in his pockets as he strolled into the house. She raised her eyebrows and glanced toward the kitchen.

His gaze darkened. "What are you doing here, Stacy?"

"Who is that?" she hissed from the other room.

"Does it matter?" His eyes flashed, all of the anger and bitterness she'd seen the other night returning full force. "It's none of your business. You dumped me a month ago, remember?"

"I obviously made the right call. Wasn't anything there if you moved on this fast," she spat, those pretty features contorting with rage. "Tell me, how long did it take until this bitch was in your bed?"

Neve rolled her eyes. Even though she wanted to be far from the middle of this, Stacy seemed determined to drag her in. "I'm some homeless girl, not his new girlfriend. Chill."

The blonde pursed her lips. "No one invited you into the conversation."

"No one invited you into my apartment either," he shot back. "Was there a point to this, or did you swing by to throw around accusations?"

The air between them sizzled, and not in a good way. She had dealt with enough crap from Veronica to know she didn't want to get in the middle of this mess. Rising from the couch, she went to the kitchen and tapped him on the shoulder. "Can I bum a smoke?"

His eyebrows scrunched together. "I didn't know you smoked."

"Neither did I." She forced a grin, letting a couple teeth poke through.

The hint of a smile snuck onto his face as he passed over his cigarettes and a lighter. Stacy watched the interchange like an android absorbing data. Neve swaggered by, blowing a kiss in Stacy's direction as she walked away. Brendan snorted. She relished the sound as she exited his apartment and clattered down the steps.

Outside, the late afternoon sun blazed, holding onto the final remnants of light before dipping below the horizon. She pulled a cigarette from the pack, staring down at the tiny cancer stick. She'd never smoked before, but the way the other waitresses at her job sucked the things down, it had to do something for the nerves.

With a flick of a Bic, the cigarette was lit. Lifting it to her lips, she sucked in. The smoke filled her lungs, and she erupted into a fit of coughing. Books had lied—this wasn't the magical stress reliever they all trumped it to be. She leaned against a car, staring at Brendan's apartment window. Poor guy hadn't closed his drapes, so he and Stacy fought on full display. She took another drag as she watched, the motion coming so naturally it surprised her.

Looks like he had his own Veronica to deal with— same blonde-haired, blue-eyed form of twit who didn't want to work and liked to cause problems. Lots of problems.

He tossed his hands in the air, and his cheeks reddened, visible even from the parking lot. Meanwhile, Stacy exuded cold ice queen. Neve let out a stream of smoke, watching as he gestured toward the door. His ex shook her head, not budging, so the fight continued.

She glanced at the cigarette's gleaming embers and flicked ashes onto the concrete. *Tap, tap.*

Brendan walked out of sight of the window, but blondie stayed planted.

Neve inhaled another drag from the cigarette, this time the smoke prickling as it filled her lungs.

When he reappeared into view, his brows furrowed. Stacy's hand flew his way, but he caught it midair and held her wrist. She lunged in, locking lips with him.

Neve let out the stream of smoke.

He pulled her off, pushing her away. Blondie balled her hands into fists. Flinging the door open, he pointed outside, and she stormed away.

Tap, tap. She flicked more ashes onto the ground.

Time to make herself scarce because, hell, she didn't want to pass that thunderhead on her way out. She continued to smoke as she circled the building, letting the rays of the sun soak into her skin. He might be a bit of an ass, but if he'd dealt with blondie long enough.... Well, she'd had experience with what that kind of people did to your personality. Give them long enough and they'd inflict permanent damage. Winding her way around the building, she glanced across the parking lot. Clear. She tossed her cigarette to the sidewalk and ground it out under her boot.

When she reached Brendan's apartment door, she knocked first. "Hey, it's me, Neve."

Seconds later, the door creaked open. His jaw clenched tight, and those blue eyes burned with their own sort of fire. He was still agitated from Stacy's visit, and why wouldn't he be? The woman had breached his personal space by waiting for him in his own apartment.

She frowned, not sure what to say to him. "Sorry your ex is a bitch" didn't slice up well if lingering feelings were involved. She decided on, "You okay?"

"Peachy," he spat, pacing the living room like the

ground was ablaze. "Did you let her in?"

"A whole lot of no. She was here when I returned from my less-than-successful attempt to get my shit from my stepmother's." She sat next to him on the couch. This sort of pissed off didn't warrant Kumbayas or talking about feelings. Aggression like this demanded slinging the first punch in a bar brawl, firing rounds at a range, or setting a car on fire. She knew—she'd been there.

She leaned into the couch cushions and stared at his blank TV. Underneath sat a console with a couple games. She crawled over to scan the titles before plucking out a Capcom fighter. "Care to play a couple rounds?"

Stopping mid-pace, he cocked his head to the side. She grinned. Distraction did work.

"You're telling me you want to play *Marvel vs. Capcom*? Right now? Out of the blue?" He approached, arms crossed and still angry.

"Well, it's either that or watch you burn holes into the carpeting with all your pacing. Me? I'd rather play a game." She put the disk in, grabbed a controller, and sat on the couch. "Come on, sucker. Prepare to eat dirt."

He blinked, a ghost of a smile returning as he swiped a controller from the floor, joining her on the couch. "Have you even played this before?"

"Please. I had no friends and pretty much either worked or hermited. Yes, I've played this before." She pursed her lips, scrolling through the characters.

They both picked their guys, and she set to work taking him down. She hadn't played in a while, but the moves came back like she'd never stopped. He wasn't shabby, though, managing to keep up.

"You're not bad." He sounded surprised.

Neve arched an eyebrow. "Yes, oh chauvinistic one, women do play video games." She scanned through the characters again, choosing her next ones. Out of the corner of her eye, she caught him watching her.

"As much as it's a normal thing, I still find a girl who can game exceedingly hot." He grinned, a crooked tooth poking out.

A flush crawled onto her cheeks as she tried to play it cool. Despite his prickliness, and even with hair mussed and a grease-stained shirt from work, he was attractive as all get out. The way he studied her like she was something special didn't help quell her blush in the slightest.

"Yeah, yeah. Pay attention so you don't keep getting your ass kicked," she murmured.

In no time, his anger melted. They hunched forward on the couch, mashing buttons while yelling empty threats at each other. She snuck a glance his way, relief and surprising warmth welling inside her chest. For the first time since her dad left, she shed off her damage and got to be a normal girl.

Chapter Seven

Neve locked the café door before beginning her trek toward Brendan's apartment. At least they'd been busy, and she made some decent tips for once. Cash which would go straight to a security deposit for an apartment. As she walked, she rummaged inside her purse for her wallet. If she planned on crashing at Brendan's again, she should attempt cooking another meal.

Someone thumped into her shoulder. Her head whipped as the force knocked her off balance, and her hand got stuck in her purse. She tumbled to the ground, hitting the cement, hard. A groan slipped past her lips as she brushed gravel off her knees where her pants had ripped.

"Neve Wynn, is that you?" a familiar voice asked.

She accepted the offered hand, focusing on the owner. His long, lean face was meticulously shaved, and brown wavy hair streaked with silver trailed down to his chin. She'd grown up seeing those warm, cocoa-brown eyes, but it had been years.

"Uncle Nate?"

The man wasn't her uncle by blood, but her father's old coworker had joined them for so many Thanksgivings she'd lost count. Nate had been a part of her life for a while, but after her mom died and her dad ran off, he'd stopped coming around. Not like she could blame him. Veronica could scare anyone away.

"I've been calling the house to get ahold of you for weeks. Why haven't you gotten back to me?" He crossed his arms over his chest.

"Considering Veronica gave me the boot, I'd have a tough time answering the house phone." She shrugged, bitterness rising in her throat again like bile.

Nate's eyebrows furrowed together. "That woman...." He growled.

"Is a problem. I agree. You can take the beef up

with my dad if you can find him." Neve gripped her purse like a lifeline. Somehow talking to him opened her wounds, scraping them raw.

He recoiled as if punched. "You mean she didn't tell you? She had to have told you."

"Told me what?" A sinking feeling reappeared in her stomach. Any news regarding her family couldn't be good.

He shook his head. "Let's talk. Do you have time? Can I buy you dinner?"

Although she wanted to head back to Brendan's and curl up on the couch with a book, her curiosity had been piqued. "Lead the way."

Minutes later, under the full blast of air conditioning in the Applebee's, she sank into the maroon pleather seating. Before they could even speak, the waitress rushed over and left with two orders for salad.

"I'm trying to watch my girlish figure. What's your damage?" Neve tried joking with Nathan to lighten the tension. He stared at her with a haunted look that creeped her out. She was at a deadlock as to whether or not she wanted to hear the news at this point.

"Vegetarian as charged." He wrung the napkin, tearing it into hundreds of tiny shreds littering the table. A heavy sigh slipped from his mouth. "Looks like I'll be the one to break it to you. About your father—" His mouth snapped shut, and those soft brown eyes watered.

She blinked at him. The air conditioning hummed in the background, the noise dominating her mind. Blaring through the restaurant, a loud synth of whatever pop trash they played crashed through. Too loud, the sounds were too loud. His mouth formed words, but she couldn't hear. Not with all that deafening noise. Tears rolled down his cheeks. She looked away, but the tacky cutouts on the walls surrounded her with bright circus colors, like some hideous carnival with all that cacophony in the background. Prickles raced over her skin. Her breath quickened. She had to shut off the music. Had to make it quiet.

Uncle Nate stared at her. "I'm sorry." He quieted with a trembling lip.

She blinked again. "I'm sorry, what?"

"He's gone. Before he could even see you again

and before he could tell you about us. I tried to get him to come down, I really did."

She clenched her jaw. None of the words coming out of his mouth painted a picture she liked.

Dad is gone. She knew that. He'd already left her. *Think. Uncle Nate said something else. Think, think, think.*

Dad is gone....

Nate means dead. He means Dad has passed away. Doesn't exist. The thought couldn't tunnel past the hole her father had created when he'd ditched her. For Neve, her father had died the day he left.

But Nate was a different matter. The realization hit her like a two-ton truck. Her father hadn't run off with a mystery man. Her father hadn't come down with a case of the gay. Uncle Nate, the guy who'd been around forever, the one who used to take her to the park and who'd bought her ice cream during her summer vacations—that's who he'd run away with.

After Veronica had kicked her out, she hadn't believed the world could knock her down more. Served her right for underestimating. Universe, two. Neve, zero. This shook her entire childhood upside down, colored it in a different light.

Her mind snapped like a rubber band, numbed over. Hell, she could barely feel her fingers curl around the fork as the waitress brought their salads.

"When's the funeral?" she asked, the words springing from her mouth.

"Well, I couldn't get in touch with you. The funeral already happened after his crash." Nathan dabbed the corners of his eyes with the napkin he'd decimated.

She chewed on her lip. "Oh."

She couldn't picture it. She couldn't fathom her father six feet under. Dead. She shoved a forkful of salad into her mouth but didn't chew.

"Are...you okay?" Nathan reached over to place a hand over hers. Guilt tugged the sides of his lips, the secret of her father's lover come to light. However, at this point in time, she didn't need more enemies. She didn't want more people to blame. He offered compassion, and she'd be stupid not to take it. If he didn't want to talk about it and could avoid dealing with their past, she could still have him in her life.

"As good as I can be." She swallowed her salad and

shoveled more in her mouth. She wasn't sure what to do. Was she supposed to be in tears, or should she drop everything, stopping to mourn the jackass who'd abandoned her? Screw him. He went and died before she got to tell him how little he meant to her, how much he'd hurt her. Maybe it made her a terrible person, but all that remained was bitterness, bad memories, and rough times.

"Where's he buried?" she asked.

Uncle Nate chased a couple stray lettuce leaves around his plate, not speaking. His eyes were red rimmed and watery, like he'd break out in tears again at any moment. A couple of stares flickered their way, and when their waitress ducked over to the hostess stand, Neve knew they'd be the topic of the day.

"Overbrook Cemetery, right by the station," he choked out, his voice thick.

She frowned. Should she comfort him? Was that weird? She reached over, placing her hand on top of his trembling one. He broke into sobs, attracting looks from everyone in the room. She opened her mouth, but, unsure of what to say, closed it again.

"You're in his will, Nevie. Veronica would've

handled it, but you turned eighteen." Uncle Nate grabbed onto his decimated napkin, trying to regain his composure. "Since she kicked you out, let's make sure you get your fair share. Can you meet me on Saturday?"

"Afternoon? I'll be at the café in the morning." She sighed, sure she had handled this loss thing wrong. When her mom had died, she'd sobbed for days. A hole had opened in her heart like someone had stabbed her in the chest, same as when her father had abandoned her. To this news, though, she was numb.

"Three, to be specific. Where are you staying? Do you need a place to crash?"

Her lip trembled at the offer. While her own flesh and blood had denied her and her father had ditched her with his mess, Uncle Nate was a different breed. She could stay with him and not worry, take her time getting a place. Brendan would be thrilled.

She gazed at her uncle and tensed. Could she handle living with him? The truth still hovered on the outskirts of her mind, filed under "refuse-to-process." Living with him, she wouldn't have any chance to avoid the reality of what had happened, and she wouldn't be able to maintain this cavalier relationship with him.

"I'm crashing on a friend's couch right now, but I'll be on my feet in no time." She offered a faint, although strained, smile.

"If you need anything, don't hesitate to ask me. Please." His voice held a note of pleading she didn't like, reminding her too much of where his guilt stemmed from. He stood and pulled out his wallet to pay for dinner. "Give me your number, and I'll let you know where to meet me for the will reading on Saturday. Make sure to show up, and we'll make Veronica pay."

Those were the first words to hit her, since revenge she could get behind. Her stepmother made number one on her list of people she hated. "I'll be there."

She got up and reached over to shake his hand. Instead, Uncle Nate threw his arms around her, enclosing her in a tight embrace. She frowned, not sure how to handle the outburst of emotion and patted his back. His collar was wet from his tears, and the mushy fabric pressed against her cheeks as he refused to let go.

Neve extricated herself from the hug, offering a wave in his direction. "See you soon, Uncle Nate."

Walking out the doors, she could sense all eyes boring down on her, but she didn't care. Let them try dealing with her mess, see how well they fared. She had something important to do, something she couldn't postpone, even if the destination set her nerves ablaze.

***

The train station appeared in the distance, the battered sign and weathered roofing not giving the greatest commendation. It wouldn't be a long hike though, just a quick, necessary stop. Neve clenched her jaw. Would take no time at all.

When the train screeched into the station, she hopped on board and slid into one of the cushioned seats, sinking in. She was tempted to skip her stop and just ride the train out. However, if she didn't go immediately, she wouldn't go at all.

Why did Nate have to find her? If he hadn't shown

up, she could've avoided this news for quite some time. She fingered the beads of her bracelet, comforted by the clink of metal on metal. Nothing she could do but keep moving forward since overnight she'd become an orphan.

The train rolled to a halt in front of Overbrook Station, and she stood. A couple of people darted off, going their separate ways the moment their feet hit concrete. She made a guess at direction before starting down the road. The hills with the tombstones jutting from them were enough of an indicator.

Amber light glowed down on the trees, one of the first signs of sunset in the fading day. Breezes brought the scent of motor oil, which clung to her like a film. She trekked down the sidewalk, heading toward the Overbrook Cemetery, which grew more expansive with each step closer. Her fingertips brushed across the wrought-iron fence as she strode through the front gates.

Despite it being the middle of the summer, patches of the grass were more of a flaccid brown than the lush green she'd expected. *Fitting for a cemetery.* Her heart hammered in her ears, and she wasn't quite sure if the sweat dripping down her neck was from the heat or nerves.

At the end of the lineup, she spotted a grave. Without even seeing the name, she knew. A firm rectangle made of sharp, finite angles—limestone and granite. The unadorned dirt lay piled in that loose, fresh-filled way. One cautious step after another, she approached. Her fingers and toes numbed. Her brain skipped like a CD refusing to bypass the scratch.

She stepped in front to face it. *In Loving Memory of Stephen Wynn*.

The words stared at her, and, before she realized, she burst into laughter. *In whose loving memory?* Not hers. Harsh, bitter laughs exploded from her like shrapnel, and she didn't care who was cut in the process. Not like she'd have to worry about much, being the sole person in the cemetery. She took a seat in front of the tombstone, sobering as fast as the hysteria had hit.

"Fuck you." Her voice cut through the thickened air. "Fuck you, Dad. I should be crying right now, you know?" She tore a handful of grass, fingers piercing into the dirt. "I should be mourning the loss of a great father, of the guy who saw me through childhood. But you screwed me over the moment Mom died."

She pushed from the ground to pace, nervous energy flooding through her. "You heard me. Since Mom died, you were absent. You were shit. You married that bitch and then decided to have a life change at the last moment, one which didn't include the family you'd created. You didn't include me." Her breath hitched as she clutched onto the tombstone.

"Daughters aren't trash you can toss away, Dad. I had to deal with the mess you left." The words hissed from her throat. "She's kicked me out, so I'm on my own. Funny thing is you could've done something. You could've done anything, and it would've been better than ditching me to move away with your boyfriend. Thanks for all the memories, Dad. Fuck you."

Tears pricked at her eyes, burning there with the pent-up hatred she'd been holding onto all these years, all she'd hoped to tell him because she wanted to hurt him. She wanted him to hurt the way he'd hurt her. But no. He had to go and kick the bucket before she could. Of course, Stephen Wynn would take the easy way out. Tears rolled down her cheeks, heating them on the way down. Salty and stinging, they burned but not like the fire inside her chest, which grew every second she stared at the grave.

She took a seat again, glaring at the tombstone. Overhead, the sky began to purple, and streaks of pink blotted across it like watercolor. The sun was setting, but Neve made no move to get up. Instead, she sat as gentle breezes dried her tears, making her cheeks stiff. The air grew colder, and each inhale became a little harsher.

As the sky faded to night, her anger dissipated— but not in a healing way, just dulled, like forged iron sizzling in a cold pail of water. Hollow. She was hollow like this place, haunted by ghosts and memories she couldn't touch.

Neve lifted her purse. Gathering herself, she walked one step at a time toward the exit. Once she reached the gates, she turned for a last look. Stephen Wynn's resting place was lost amidst all the stones, another rock stuck in the ground.

Forgotten.

Chapter Eight

Work at the café passed in a blur. Neve managed minimal interaction despite her customer-oriented job. As she approached the apartment door, she tugged on the spiked collar around her throat, hoping Brendan had found something else to do on a Friday evening. Taking a deep breath, she entered.

He sat on the couch, relaxing with his hands behind his head. He glanced her way and flashed a grin, his eyes crinkling with a warmth that surprised her. She licked her dry lips.

"What were you doing last night?" He turned his focus to the TV. "Finding an apartment, I hope."

"Don't lie, you know you missed me." She nudged him out of the way as she took a seat next to him on the couch. Everything from the day before remained stitched tight in her mind—as if one thread came loose she'd unravel.

"Counting off the days until you leave, Neve Wynn." The hint of a smile that flickered to his face gave him away. "I'm planning on going to the diner, though, if you'd like to join."

"A Friday night and you're spending it at that infernal diner?" She jostled him with her elbow.

He pushed back, and a wide grin broke out on his face. "Yeah, like you don't want to go."

"Caught me. I guess I'm as lame as you." Grabbing her purse, she made her way to the door. "So, how quick can you get ready?"

***

Neve's stomach ached—she hadn't touched anything since the salad the day before, but she wasn't sure she could eat. Nothing like finding out about your estranged dad's death to throw your appetite out the window.

The Cottage Diner's homey lights glowed onto

black asphalt which just sucked up the beams to spit out more shadows. Approaching the glass doors with Brendan felt right, a comfortable routine already—which was something she couldn't afford, not when everything she touched turned to shit.

She bit down on her lower lip, wishing she could rewind yesterday and avoid running into Uncle Nate. Her grip tightened on the railing as they strode to the door. Daydreams were dangerous, insidious, because once she found a new apartment, all of this would end.

"Hey, Space Queen, you there?" Brendan held the door for her.

Nodding, she walked inside, not bothering to explain. At the corner table sat Martin, this time in a starched button-down with his hair combed back. Colin had wedged in next to him, leaning on a stack of textbooks and looking exhausted. In the corner sat a tall, muscled guy who was military buff with a complementary buzz cut.

"How many more of you are there? It's like stepping into a cabal of dwarves." She rolled her eyes as she slid in next to Martin.

"I object to the use of cabal," Colin murmured from behind his stack of books. "Horde could fit. Maybe tribe. And the only one who's uncouth enough to be a dwarf is Jared here."

So, new guy had a name. Jared gave her a grin, his white teeth gleaming against his tanned skin. "Gabe told me a broad started showing up. A goth chick."

She raised an eyebrow. "Is that what I am? I guess black hair and pale skin is the recipe for insta-goth."

Brendan nudged her, sitting beside her. The simple action pierced the first tendril of warmth through the hollowness aching inside. But getting close to anyone wasn't in her plan, not when she was this messed up.

"Your luck beginning to turn around?" Martin asked as Jennie came by with cups of coffee for the table.

Neve took a long sip of hers. Christ, she didn't even know how to respond. A lie would be smart since it would hide the awkwardness of what had happened. But she'd already paused too long for anything but the truth.

Brendan's gaze heated her—she could sense him

watching. Jared stared her way, along with Martin, both waiting for a response.

"Let's say I'm due for some good news."

"What happened yesterday?" He placed a hand on her shoulder, a gesture that surprised her.

"Got some bad news from an old family friend." Sighing, she blew off some of the steam curling from her coffee. With the attention on her, all she could do to keep her mind together was gaze at her reflection in the dark liquid.

"Woman, how much more bad news can you receive? You've already been kicked out of your house, don't have a mom—" Colin looked up from above his books. "Something happened to your dad, didn't it?"

Who said men aren't perceptive? She gulped down the coffee, ignoring the scorching on the roof of her mouth. The acid felt right in her stomach, adding to the bitter hollowness aching there.

"Gee, Sherlock, solved the puzzle already?" She tucked a couple stray strands of hair behind her ear. "Yeah, my dad kicked the bucket." The second the words left her mouth, Martin's face dropped and

Colin's glasses slid down his nose. Brendan squeezed her shoulder, but she couldn't deal with the intensity in his gaze. "Not a big deal, guys. I wrote him off the day he ditched my family."

The table grew pin-drop silent.

She let out a frustrated huff. "Not awkward unless you make it awkward. Guys, I'm fine."

Martin recovered his poise first. "Man, I apologize for asking. Let us know if you need anything."

"See? Goth." Jared nodded her way. She couldn't tell whether his smile was mocking or not.

"What, because I'm an orphan? Tell that to Bruce Wayne." Like she needed some meathead judging her because of the shit course her life had taken. There was nothing tragic about her father's death—the asshole had just managed to find another way to duck out of parenting.

"She referenced Batman, Brendan. Have you proposed yet?" Colin pushed his glasses up on his nose.

"Too much competition, what with his ex," she interjected, offering Brendan an extra-sweet smile. He shot her daggers.

Martin shook his head. "Stacy's still in the picture? Bren, do us a favor and clean break it. Cut her out."

"In his defense, she did break into his apartment." She sipped from her coffee again, grateful the attention had moved away from her.

"I'm done sitting back." Jared slammed his fist on the table, sending droplets of Neve's coffee to splash onto her wrist. "If you don't put a restraining order out on the bitch, I will."

Brendan sighed. "Look, I know I need to take some stronger measures in making sure she stays out. But it's my business, and I'll handle it." He gave her a look, making her feel guilty for bringing it up in the first place. She'd been trying to distract everyone from her crap but, instead, aired his drama.

Martin's focus shifted to the door, his lip curling like he'd swallowed something sour.

She turned around, following his line of sight. "Looks like she wants to make it everyone else's business."

A tall, shapely, blonde missile headed their way.

Brendan's jaw tightened even though he hadn't bothered to look. His grip on his coffee cup was half a squeeze away from shattering it.

Stacy stopped in front of the table, her arms crossed and teeth set as she stared down Neve. This week had taken a memo to fling shit at her in whatever way possible.

"Yeah, and you aren't dating. What's she doing here with you? Already bringing her out with the guys?" Her voice echoed in the near-empty diner.

Martin winced. Colin ducked behind his books, and Jared tensed with his palms flat on the table, half-ready to bolt.

Brendan stared at his cup of coffee, rage filling his eyes. Every muscle from his neck to his arms went taut.

Yeah, he's pissed. And barely containing it. She glanced around. *Seems all these guys have some history with this girl. But I don't.* She had no reason to be nice, and, after the hellish week she'd had, charitable wasn't on her to-do list. *Stacy wants to target me? Tough shit. I'm not gonna play her games.*

"Leave," Neve said, her voice low.

"Who are you to tell me what to do?" Stacy set her

hands on her hips.

"You're near shouting in a public place, trying to cause shit with your ex, and when he won't bite, trying to start shit with a stranger. Check yourself. It's embarrassing." She stayed level, calm. She took a sip of coffee, not wanting to gauge the reaction on the blonde's face.

Brendan's hand shot out in front of her, almost causing her to drop the cup. His fingers wrapped around Stacy's wrist right before she could knock into Neve's coffee. *He has reflexes like a cat. Thank Christ, too, because the confrontation would've gotten nasty.*

"Stacy, you've got every right to go wherever you want, but no right to be rude to my friends or cause a scene." His voice was steel, and his fingers didn't budge around her wrist. She tugged, but he held tight.

"I don't hit women, but if you don't leave my boy alone, I'll make an exception," Jared growled. "Get the hell out."

Stacy's lip quivered. Bursting into tears, she stormed off, her loud stomping sending stares their way. Neve wrapped both hands around her coffee cup and sighed.

"Has she gotten so low to track you down to where you're hanging out?" Disgust marred Martin's face.

"Maybe she'll piss off now." Brendan's jaw tensed—he seemed ready to burn holes into the table. "I told her I didn't want her around, and I meant it, but I guess she lingered once she realized breaking up with me meant her meal ticket had vanished."

"I think Neve and Jared scared her enough." Colin smirked, taking a bite out of his egg salad sandwich.

"Goth girl, where'd you get those cojones?" Jared drawled, casting a lazy glance her way, one bordering on a leer.

Ugh, she preferred his disinterest. "I'm emotionless, didn't you hear? A robot, pretty much. My dad kicked the bucket, and you don't see me crying."

"I wish you would've told me before we left." Brendan's face sank into his hands, his fingers digging into his skull. "Maybe I could've avoided my psycho ex. Either way, I think I'm calling it a short night tonight." He gave her a side glance. "Care to join?"

She ignored the heat rising to her cheeks as Martin's eyebrows lifted high. Whatever the guys thought, it wasn't like that—they weren't like that. Even though he was the one person who sparked anything inside her—mostly frustration—the hellish past couple of days had scooped her hollow. "Yeah, I could use a drink."

"Corrupting minors now, are we?" Colin teased.

Brendan snorted and threw down the money for his coffee. Waving at the guys, she followed him out of the diner.

***

"Do another shot with me." Neve slammed her fist on the coffee table.

He'd pulled out a handle of whisky once they'd reached the apartment, and everything had gone downhill from there. After all, the perfect way to dull the ache inside her chest was to fill it with warmth— whisky sufficed.

Brendan grinned, speaking more freely than he

had since they met. "Woman, we've already done too many. Take a backseat so you won't be vomiting all over my beautiful carpet."

She snorted and gave him a playful shove. "That ol' mess? It'd enhance the look."

He raised his eyebrows. "Well, well, now the truth comes flying out."

God, the way his crooked tooth pokes out with his smile. Her heart raced. The intensity in his gaze when he focused on her—she couldn't stop the flush from hitting her cheeks every time.

He lounged on the couch, hands behind his head. Something blared on the TV even though they'd stopped paying attention hours ago. She paused from ambling around the room, bottle of whisky in her hand. *The couch looks glorious.*

"Make some space, chump." She gave him a mischievous grin as she plopped beside him, draping her leg over his. To her surprise, his arm snaked around her shoulders.

"How the hell do you do it?" he asked, staring at the wall. "I mean your dad just died.... How can you be okay?"

"Well, it helps he abandoned me. All my mourning business happened then." She shrugged, staring into the bottle of whisky.

"I've never seen strength like yours." His voice had a hushed quality to it, making her flush. "Anyone else and they'd be crumpled in a corner right now."

His words made her mind reel, but her insides hurt. Kindness wasn't something she could handle. "Nah, I'm just heartless. That's all."

Hips pressed together, legs on one another's, and his arm around her—she shivered from the warmth. This close to him, she could smell the whisky on his breath and the slight pine scent of his aftershave. She wanted more. More warmth and more of him, anything to get rid of the emptiness inside her aching like bitter winter winds.

She snuck a glance at him. His eyes were half-closed, revealing long lashes any girl would kill for. Damn guy had an olive complexion to hide the effects of the whisky, unlike her pale skin. Cuddled with him like this, his lips inches away, the curiosity of how he'd taste held her mind in a vise. She lifted the bottle to her lips and took another swig, placing it on the coffee table afterward.

The lingering way he watched her drove her nuts. She didn't know whether she wanted to punch him or kiss him, but this very moment, she needed to feel something beyond all the numbness. Instead of leaning into the couch, she twisted around on top of him. She straddled him, her fingertips burying into his hair and then trailing down his neck. Screw the repercussions, and screw this space between them. She wanted to lose herself in his warmth.

He cupped her cheek, staring at her with wonder, making her feel vulnerable—too close to something real.

She leaned in, her lips brushing against his.

"Neve," he said, his voice throaty and hoarse. "Stop."

The illusion shattered. All the warmth, all the whisky, and all the coziness froze.

"Your dad died, and I'd be a dick to take advantage of you while you're drunk and hurting."

She pulled away at once, embarrassment burning her cheeks. The room spun from the quick motion while her stomach tightened. The fragile tension between them crumbled, and she pushed off of him, sliding as far away as possible on the couch. Screw him, his morals, and his self-righteousness for making her feel this way. No one wanted her anyway. Why should he?

Pulling her knees to her chest, she stared down at her feet, unwilling to meet his gaze. Seconds later, the cushion moved as he rose from the couch, and a blanket found its way around her shoulders.

"Sweet dreams," he slurred as he stumbled off to his room.

Her embarrassment worsened the ache in her chest, stirring old memories better left alone. As she clutched the blanket, she stared out the window, the glow of the streetlamps swirling from her shaky vision and the moonlight counting the hours for her.

Chapter Nine

As she walked down the sidewalk, Neve glanced at her reflection in the windows. Between the bags under her eyes and her mussed hair, she made quite the picture. Thank everything holy Brendan had still been asleep when she'd left for work.

When she remembered the mess she'd made the night before, her chest tightened. This morning, he'd been another embarrassment to avoid. The rest of the day held more awkwardness—of the family variety. Uncle Nate had sent her the address for Thomas Delaney, Attorney at Law, and today marked the first time she would see Veronica since she'd given her the boot on her birthday. She didn't expect anything from the father who had abandoned her, but she went to make sure her stepmother didn't screw her over more than she already had. The chance to take her down a peg would be its own reward.

Today had shaped up to be dismal, and Neve imagined it would get worse. The pelting rain didn't help her pounding head in the slightest, either. Drops of water washed over crushed Starbucks cups and slid off of plastic Wawa bags to form puddles on the ground. She spotted the office in the distance, clear by the shoe-polish black sign with the gold engraving of Thomas Delaney and Associates. Appearing like a wet dog wasn't the best way to enter into battle, but sans umbrella and with the rain beginning to pour, that was how she would arrive.

Her heart rate increased, the same way it had on returning to her home the other day. No matter how tough she told herself she was, the thought of dealing with Veronica regressed her to a scared little kid. She clutched her purse in a death grip before striding to the front door.

As she stepped inside, the scent of polished wood and new carpet flooded her nose. A secretary dressed in a pressed suit sat behind a slick black desk, ignoring the ringing phone while she attacked the stacks of paper around her.

"Excuse me." Neve's voice came off louder than ever in the silent office.

"Here for the will of Steven Wynn?" The woman analyzed her with sharp, dark eyes.

"Uh, yeah." Her throat tightened. Here she stood in the offices where Veronica, Uncle Nate, and the will of her father would battle it out. Like usual, she would be passed around, dealt cards, and have to make do.

"Right through the door." The woman pointed, already returning her attention to her desk.

The frosted-glass entry revealed dark blobs moving around on the opposite side. Before she could open the door, it swung open, revealing an older man, shaven with a trim suit, who she assumed was Thomas Delaney.

"Neve Wynn?" he asked.

"Guilty." She stepped inside. Her attention shifted, honing in on the primped blonde woman in a business suit with the frost-queen face. *Veronica.*

Uncle Nate walked over, cutting through her

vision of her stepmother. Even though his face still clung to that pallor, he looked much more put together than the last time she saw him. Today, his gelled hair was slicked back, and he wore a tailored suit elevating him to ten times sharper than the average shark. He and Veronica had both dressed to be taken seriously. Neve glanced down at her wet camo pants, black wife-beater, and dark-gray hoodie. *Oh, well.*

Delaney pulled a seat out. "It's time to discuss the matter of Stephen Wynn's will."

Taking the cue, she sat down, trying to ignore Veronica's cold gaze. Uncle Nate leaned over and squeezed her shoulder. Even though the gesture was sweet, she fought the hair-trigger impulse to deck him.

Thomas Delaney peered over the papers, his bushy brows casting shade over his gaze and hiding his boredom. "He has certain personal items delegated to individuals, but we'll start with the larger assets."

Veronica held her chin high, confidence beaming from her self-righteous smile. Neve's jaw tightened. *She must know something the rest of us don't. This was a waste of time.* If she had to sit there and watch Veronica assume possession of her childhood house, it'd be another slap in the face from her father, posthumously.

"As a token of gratitude for watching over his daughter, Stephen Wynn delegated the household possessions to Veronica Renard."

"And what about the house itself?" A blonde brow lifted as her voice sharpened.

"Stephen Wynn has designated Nathan Gregory as the recipient of his home in Berwyn."

Neve let out a snort. *Bet she didn't anticipate that.* She snuck a glance, satisfied to see the white pallor on her ex-stepmother's face.

"You must be reading it wrong." Veronica crossed her arms over her chest.

A hint of a smile spread onto Uncle Nate's face as he leaned over to pat her on the shoulder. "Tough luck, darling. Guess he liked me a bit more."

Veronica's nails dug into the chair arms, but she didn't say anything to Uncle Nate. Neve sighed. She wasn't sure why she'd even bothered to come. While seeing Veronica taken down a peg gave her some satisfaction, it still didn't solve any of her problems. The whole will reading reminded her of how little her dad had cared about her.

"As for his main financials, those will be going to Nathan Gregory," Delaney continued.

She fidgeted in her seat, picking at the wood grain on the chair arms. The pit in her stomach had continued to grow ever since she'd run into Uncle Nate the other day, a swallow of foreboding and futility. This week had been a long dark one with no light at the end of the tunnel.

"With the exception of a sum of ten thousand dollars, designated for Neve Wynn," Delaney read off.

She tilted her head, not quite understanding. "I think you misread."

Uncle Nate squeezed her shoulder again. "Not in the slightest. You're his daughter. He'd be a fool not to leave something to you."

Right. The chances of Stephen Wynn doing something considerate on his own, she doubted. However, with some promptings from Uncle Nate.... Despite the role he might've played in her past, he had good intentions when it came to her.

Ten thousand. She couldn't even fathom that amount of money. It meant she could afford to get her apartment. Get out of Brendan's hair and their whole awkward situation. Her shoulders relaxed, the tension melting down her arms like warm honey.

"This can't be the right will," Veronica stated, voice sharp as a razor as she stared down Delaney. "I was his wife, who he abandoned with his child. There must be a clause for taking her in."

"Ma'am, this is the will for Stephen Wynn. Maybe you aren't Veronica Renard, or you're sitting in for the wrong will reading, but this is the correct document. I can guarantee." Delaney placed the papers on the desk and fixed the woman with the full force of his weary gaze.

"You're telling me my current home is forfeit?" She bolted from her seat, hands balled into fists. All the fancy suits and expensive purses in the world wouldn't help her against a piece of paper.

"I'm not telling you anything except what's here. As for individual items, they'll be delivered. With the major assets delegated, you are all free to go."

"Calm down, Veronica." Uncle Nate straightened

his lapels. "I have a place of my own in the city and no desire to move down here. I'll be putting the house up for sale, so you'll have time to find a place of your own." His eyebrows lowered. "More time than you gave Neve."

"I should've known you had something to do with this." Her stepmother's sugar-sweet voice held acid bitterness beneath it.

Neve grinned. "I've got no clue what you're talking about."

Veronica took in a deep inhale, venom radiating from her pores as she stared down all of them. "This has been an utter waste of time, from the second I met that asshole father of yours to the years I spent taking care of your ungrateful ass. I've had enough."

Turning on her heel, she strode out the frosted-glass door, letting it slam behind her. Neve winced at the reverberations.

"Don't worry, the glass is strong for a reason," Delaney murmured as he sat behind his desk, already leafing through a separate pile of papers.

Uncle Nate snorted, placing an arm around her. She resisted the urge to shrug him off, reminding herself human contact was a good thing. Having an ally in her corner would serve her better in the long run than pushing everyone away.

"I think we need a redo on lunch. The other day was too much, me dropping this news on you." Uncle Nate led her out the door and toward the entrance. "Let's focus on the future, on finding you an apartment."

***

Neve marched up the squeaky steps of Brendan's apartment building. The overhead fluorescents kept flickering, lights needing repair since before she'd arrived. Lunch with Uncle Nate had turned into a game of avoiding the obvious. They'd managed to keep the topics light while they focused on trying to find her an apartment—even narrowed it down to a couple of local listings. *Time to launch from that to facing Brendan.*

With his tight body, all his warmth, and the way his arm had curled around her.... She bit her lower lip. Last night she'd been hoping for a distraction and made a misstep. Better to just pretend that whole mess never happened and pray he would avoid talking about it. Pushing open the door, she walked inside.

He sat on the couch, attention focused on a book. A strand of hair had fallen across his forehead, and those blue eyes were intense while he pored over whatever he read.

Like he could get any hotter. Forget his warmth. Forget his pine-scented aftershave. Struggling to ignore the knot in her chest, she strolled into the living room.

"Long time no see." He looked up from his book and smiled. "Where were you all day?"

Her heart skipped a couple beats at the sight of him. *Drat.* Her own body betrayed her. "Dealing with the will of the late Stephen Wynn. Lovely family reunion with Veronica. All too touching." She managed to maintain a monotone, but her stomach squeezed at her words. She still couldn't fathom her father six feet under, even though she'd divorced herself from him the day he'd abandoned her.

"Ah, sorry to hear." He set his book down and

made space for her on the couch.

She took a seat so as not to be rude, but it twisted her more having him this close and not being able to do anything about it. He would reject her again, chalking it up to the grief she wasn't feeling over her dad's death.

"Don't be. I got a lump sum from the old man which'll get me out of here by the end of the week." She watched him, his expression unreadable. "See? I'm no slouch. So much for all the judgment you slung my way," she teased.

"Maybe some of it was misplaced." A smirk rose to his lips.

"Want to order pizza? I'm starving, and it's my treat."

"Now you're speaking my language." He grabbed a folder of menus from under the coffee table. Their hands brushed as she reached for one marked pizzeria, and he stopped, placing his over hers. The second their eyes met, she froze in place, caught in the storm of his gaze. "You realize all the crap I said was bitterness over Stacy, right? Having you here hasn't been an inconvenience. My place has been a little less lonely for the first time in a long while."

The tension between them charged the air until she couldn't pull away, didn't want to—even though she should. Deep down, he was soft, warm, and real, but her? She was hollow on the inside. The ache couldn't be filled by some happy relationship, not when damaged girl brought more misery on everything and everyone around her. His lips were so inviting—just as they had been the other night—but no way would she make the same mistake again. Rejection burned a deep enough brand to keep her from repeating.

His phone buzzed, ripping through the quiet like a chainsaw.

"Going to get that?" she asked as it continued to ring.

"Nope, don't recognize the number, so they can leave a message." Snatching his phone, he tucked it in his pocket.

"Right, then." She pulled out her own phone. "Pizza?"

Chapter Ten

Neve sank her teeth into the diner burger, the dripping juices streaming down her fingers as she devoured it. Tonight, Jared, Gabe, and Conor had put in an appearance— Martin had a date. Brendan took his seat next to her like always, muddling her feelings all the more.

"God, food never tasted so good," Jared said through an open mouthful of fries.

"Please, for all our sakes, contain yourself." She placed her cheeseburger on the plate and gave him an extra-sweet smile. He threw daggers her way.

"To think we met you a week ago." Gabe grinned as he speared fries with his fork, mashing them into his plate.

"Longest week of my life." She tried to maintain a

serious face but couldn't keep from breaking into a grin again. Despite her hellish family situation and the confusion with Brendan, she loved these diner nights. However, once she left his couch, there was no guarantee those would continue.

"So stud, how did your date last night go?" Jared winked, focusing his attention on Brendan.

She narrowed her eyes. What was Jared referring to? Had he considered their hanging out and grabbing pizza a date?

"Didn't go." He focused on his plate, not glancing her way.

The knot in her chest returned stronger than ever. Whenever she got her hopes up, life found a way to crush them.

"Ridiculous. Liz is smoking hot. Puts Stacy to shame. Blonde hair, perfect tits, and legs that stretch for miles. If you didn't want her, I would've taken a spin." Jared gave him a wicked grin. The tip of his tongue darted over his teeth, and those stretched triceps exuded machismo. Not her type in the slightest, but she could see how some girls would go for him.

"Yeah, didn't pan out." Brendan still hadn't looked her way, dancing around the subject as though he had something to hide. Not like she relished talking about all the hot chicks banging on his door. With her pale skin, dark hair, and well, goth look, she didn't hold a candle to Stacy or any other all-American gal.

Her appetite vanishing, she pushed her burger away.

"In other words, he chickened out." Conor reached over like he was going to pat Brendan on the shoulder. Instead, he snatched his phone and began scrolling through his numbers. "However, as your dear concerned friends who don't want you to get back with Stacy, let's handle this efficiently."

He made a grab for his phone, but Conor swerved out of the way, typing something. Neve swallowed, trying to stay flippant and ignore the black pit opening in her stomach. She'd known when he turned her down the other night he wasn't interested, but it hurt a whole different way to see girls compete for a guy who, despite his grade-A personality defects, made her heart race.

"Dude, give it to me. I didn't want to go on the

date, so leave it be." He groped forward, still trying to wrest the phone from Conor.

The guy returned it, a saccharine smile on his lips. "Fine."

Brendan slumped forward, scrolling through his texts. "Why don't I trust you?" He paused, reading something on the screen. "I need a cigarette." He strode out of the diner.

"What did you send? Tell me, tell me." Gabe bounced on his seat.

"An apology and make-it-up-to-you text to your Liz girl." Conor played with the cuff on his sleeve, re-folding it.

Jared rose from his seat then slid next to Neve, slipping his arm around her shoulders. "Right? The boy has issues. He's been living with this pretty young thing for a week, and I bet he hasn't even tried to tap it."

"Hey, bucko. You do realize I'm right here?" She settled into his arm, letting the heat from his body flood against her. While he didn't make her heart race, he also didn't make it ache—casual might not be too bad.

"Oh, sweetheart, you're right where I want you." He gave her a wink.

She rolled her eyes. "Save the sugar for some other girl. This one's had it up to here with people in general."

"A challenge. I can appreciate that." He pulled her in closer. She didn't miss the way he glanced at her cleavage, on full display with her low-cut mauve tee. "You do realize you're not getting rid of me now."

"Joy." She took a long, weary sip of her coffee.

Brendan stalked inside, his cloud of smoke following him. His hand paused on the seat, ready to swing in next to her, but hesitated when his gaze landed on Jared who sat in his spot. For a moment, his fingers curled around the seat backing, but then he moved to the other side to sit next to Conor.

"If you need a place to stay, you know my bed's always welcome," Jared continued.

Neve couldn't help but notice the way Brendan stared at them, his blue eyes turning a steel gray. If looks could stab—well, his would.

"Didn't I tell you? I'll be getting my own apartment. I'll have a big, cozy bed there of my own where I can strip down and sleep naked every night." If Jared wanted to play games, she could hold her own. Brendan didn't seem too keen on her joke and turned away.

"Don't be mad about Liz." Conor placed an arm around his shoulder, shaking him a bit. "I did it for you."

"No, it was good you sent the text," he announced to the table. She didn't miss the way his glance stopped on her. "After all, how often do you meet a girl that hot?"

She clenched her jaw. *Jackass.* She had wasted her time pining over him. Annoyance flushed her cheeks. She leaned against Jared, sending a spiteful glare Brendan's way.

"It's getting pretty warm in here." She pressed her hand over her chest, tugging at the fabric clinging tight to her breasts. Sliding her hand along the side of her neck, she reached to twirl a strand of hair around her finger. Jared watched her the entire time.

"Take it off!" Gabe shouted, his grin even wider.

"This isn't a strip club." Conor hooked an arm around Gabe's neck. "Am I relegated as your handler while Martin's out?"

Jared took a generous glance down her cleavage and squeezed her tighter, so they were pressed against each other, her head leaning against his chest. Brendan's jaw tightened. If he wanted to be a jerk, she could dish it right back.

"I'm feeling kind of sick." Brendan pushed his coffee away. "I think I'm going to head out." His gaze caught hers, the question in them clear of whether or not she would join.

"You just got here," Gabe whined.

Neve pressed her tongue against the back of her teeth. After he made those jabs, she wasn't too keen on heading home right yet, not if it meant sitting at his apartment in awkward silence. "I'm going to hang out a bit more." She kept her voice light. "Would you leave the door open for me?"

"If he's not willing to give you a place to sleep, the offer of my bed's still available," Jared added in, not helping the powder keg of a situation in the slightest. The poor guy seemed oblivious to the entire battle going on across the table. Brendan's gaze grew darker, and he sucked in a deep breath before swiping his check off the counter.

"I'll be heading home, then." Instead of saying good-bye to anyone, he walked off to pay then ducked out the door.

"I'd prefer a couch any day." She leveled him with a half-lidded stare. "Come on, buddy. Is this the stuff you use on girls in the bar?"

Conor snorted, and Jared exclaimed, offering some sort of defense. But Neve's attention had gone elsewhere. Through the diner's wide windows, she spotted Brendan striding away, his shoulders squared and hood up—the same way she'd met him. He turned toward his apartment, disappearing into the darkness.

***

As she turned the knob to his apartment, Neve readied herself. Annoyance still prickled under the surface, but she'd cooled down a lot since their verbal tennis match at the diner. With any luck, he'd gone to sleep so she could sneak onto the couch and shut out the world.

She entered the apartment to lights still on and Brendan sitting on the couch. He focused on his book but this time didn't acknowledge her. The ember from his cigarette glowed orange where it perched on the ashtray. She decided to screw the awkwardness in the face by sitting beside him. Grabbing the cigarette, he took a deep drag, letting the smoke filter around the room.

"Manage to ride Jared while you were climbing on top of his lap?" The bitterness was as thick as the smoke pouring from his lips. "Just a forewarning, he's got a new girl in his bed every night. In case you were hoping for something more permanent."

Her temper boiled, ready to pour over. The nerve he had, throwing accusations when he had dates lined up, exes hanging out in his kitchen, and who knew how many other women waiting to jump his bones. Meanwhile, the one time they got close, he'd chosen to push her away.

"What makes you think I want something permanent? And you're one to talk. I was surprised I didn't come back to find some bimbo here with you."

"So what if I brought a girl home? This is my

damn apartment." He slammed the book onto his coffee table, the cigarette hanging from his lips.

"Don't worry, you haven't let me forget. I'll be out of here before you can blink." She crossed her arms over her chest and thrust her chin up. Whatever she'd felt toward him must've been a side effect of grief and stress. He was a damned irritating, annoying jackass of a man.

A stream of smoke flew from his lips as his eyes flashed with anger. "You sure you don't want to head on over to Jared's bed? Didn't see you refusing his offer."

"At least he would accept my offer, unlike some people I can think of." The hole in her chest kept growing larger and larger. Her eyes burned, but she wouldn't give him the satisfaction of seeing her cry. Of seeing how he'd burrowed under her skin.

He opened his mouth. After floundering for a couple seconds, he shut his mouth and took another drag. The heat and fury deflated from him like a hissing balloon. His lips formed a thin line as he ground out his cigarette in the ashtray.

"I'm going to bed. Good night." Seconds later, he

closed the door, disappearing into his room.

Grabbing the butt from the ashtray, she gripped the filter and tried to suck a drag out of it, tugging at the dying embers with all her might. Feeble smoke filled her lungs, but she inhaled it before dropping the smashed cigarette back into the ashtray. Lying on the couch, her arms tucked behind her head, she stared at the ceiling. She released the breath of smoke in a thin stream that trickled into the air until it grew more and more sparse. Until it vanished.

Chapter Eleven

The moment she stepped inside the apartment with Uncle Nate, she knew it would be hers. With tan walls, tan ceilings, and dark hardwood floors, the place felt warm and lived-in, even without any furniture. Much better than the white-on-white prison Veronica had turned her home into.

"If your...." The landlady squinted at Uncle Nate. She was an older woman with round glasses and frizzy hair pulled into a messy bun. "*Uncle* here will co-sign, the place is yours. All I require is my rent on time and you don't trash the place. None of those crazy parties kids your age have."

"Speaking as someone who's never been to those crazy parties you're referencing, I think we'll be okay." Neve grinned, trying to hide her excitement.

Uncle Nate squeezed her shoulder, beaming like...well, like a proud father. The dark reminder almost dampened her mood, but the landlady continued, snapping her out of it.

"Well then, if we head down to my apartment, we can sign some paperwork. I've got your keys there. Since rent's due on the first of the month, a week from now, you can move in whenever—once you give me the first month's payment and security deposit." The woman hobbled around the empty room, the floorboards creaking when she walked. As they moved through room after room, the lady flicked off the lights.

"That would be amazing," Neve whispered, barely believing how fast everything was happening. A place of her own. It'd be a thousand times better than living with Veronica, and, on her own, she might be able to make a name for herself other than "damaged girl".

"Without any furniture?" Nate squinted at her. She shrugged, and he placed his arm around her shoulders. "I've got some stuff stored away that I can send you. It might take a couple weeks, but we'll get you set up. Let's get going." He took the lead, heading out of the apartment and down the stairs.

She matched pace with the old landlady, still stunned she would have her own place tonight. A future she couldn't fathom crept into her brain as she descended, step-by-step, toward her new lease.

***

As Neve approached apartment B-07, a weight descended on her shoulders. This should be easy. After all, she'd only been at his place for a week. However, in that one week she'd been through the grinder. From the moment she met those guys at the diner, her life had never been the same. For the first time, she had found somewhere she belonged, and a big part was due to Brendan's kindness the night she'd been cast out. He'd taken her in and given her a couch to sleep on when no one else would. Despite the frustration between them, she would never forget what he'd done for her.

The dusky hues of sunset lit his apartment, similar to the amber lights lining the walls of her new place.

Even though she didn't spot him in the main living area, from the sizzle in the kitchen and smell of bacon wafting her way, she knew he was home.

"Hey," she called as she strode into the kitchen. "I've got some great news."

He stood by the stovetop, tending a skillet full of bacon and another of scrambled eggs. "Before you say anything, let me get this out. I stepped over the line with the Jared stuff, and I'm sorry."

"I am, too." She took a seat at the table. "Sorry for the jabs about the girls."

A tense silence descended on the room. She fidgeted with the strap on her bag.

"Dinner?" he offered, gesturing to the breakfast foods he prepped.

"A peace offering of bacon is always welcome." She winked, taking a seat at the table. "And as for the news, I found an apartment."

His eyebrows rose. "So fast?" He directed the scrambled eggs and bacon onto plates already laden with buttered toast. "That didn't take long."

"Like I said, I'm no slouch. Now, you'll have to call me something other than homeless girl," she teased.

The silence returned as did the heavy air of regret through the room, like watching a gorgeous sunrise fade into a gray day. He brought the food to the table, but, even with the delicious scent of bacon, butter, and skillet grease, her appetite had diminished. Still, she forked up her scrambled eggs, shoving the best bits into her mouth.

"When are you moving in?" he asked through bites of bacon.

"Tonight." She didn't lift her gaze from the plate because she didn't want to see his reaction. If he was happy, she'd be crushed. If he was sad...well, she wouldn't know how to handle sadness either. "But hey, even though I'm moving doesn't mean you've gotten rid of me at the diner."

"You're like a cockroach."

"That's me, one of the roaches." Neve jabbed a thumb at herself while nibbling her toast. Every glance she stole at Brendan felt like a final one—ridiculous since her move placed her a mere ten minutes away. Finished, she grabbed his plate and hers, taking them to the sink.

Surveying her space from the last week, she didn't

have anything to worry about packing. Veronica had taken care of most of her stuff. Everything she owned was inside her suitcase, the same one she had arrived with. The brass key weighed down her pocket, a reminder of her new home.

Even though she had to leave, she hadn't wanted to go like this—unresolved, with the heaviness of everything they never got to say suspended in the air. When they met a week or so from now, it would be at the diner, with everyone else. She wasn't the type of girl he called for a date, just the type he grabbed pizza with after a shitty night. She wrapped her fingers around the handle of her suitcase and lifted her gaze to meet his.

"You better be visiting me in my new digs." She placed one hand on her hip, brooking no refusal.

He gave her a soft smile, one of the few genuine she'd ever received. "You know you can't keep me away."

If she didn't go this second, she never would—not if she lost herself any farther into those eyes. She stuck her hand out, offering a shake. "Thank you, for everything. Things could've gone a very different way, but because of you.... Well, I get a new start. A chance to try and get things right."

He cocked an eyebrow at her. Brushing her hand aside, he threw his arms around her, squeezing her tight. Her body pressed against his and, for one brief second, she allowed herself the thrill. The scent of pine and the heat from his body...everything sent her mind reeling. But she couldn't let herself get attached, not when she was leaving. She sighed as she pulled away.

"See you later, guy from the diner." She set off down the corridor.

"See you soon, girl with the apartment," he called out, his voice carrying down the hallway and following her like a memory.

Chapter Twelve

Since Neve waited on the furniture Uncle Nate had promised, the decorating of the apartment had gone nowhere. She hadn't been to the diner in a week and hadn't seen Brendan since the night she left. The loner behaviors she'd learned as a teen lurked around the corner, waiting to ensnare her again. She'd found a home for the couple of books she still owned—lining them along the wall so they leaned into a corner of the room. A thick blanket and a pillow lay piled on her floor, but she hadn't gotten as far as a mattress yet. All in all, the apartment was barren, but hers.

With the sun already setting and no forthcoming invitation to the diner, she didn't feel comfortable enough to join the guys on her own. Looked to be another night in for her—which was fine. She had work in the morning anyway and shouldn't be out late. She pulled one of her library books from out of her purse and leaned against the wall.

The doorbell rang.

She set her book down before rising from the floor. Who would be visiting her? She'd had lunch with Uncle Nate the other day and he'd made no mention. As for the guys at the diner, none of them had her new address as far as she knew. No one except for Brendan. Her heartbeat increased a couple notches even as she scolded herself to calm down. Chances were some neighbor had a complaint about something.

No point getting her hopes up, but she still finger-combed her hair and checked her teeth in her purse mirror before opening the door.

Bedraggled blonde hair, a makeup-free face, and a wrinkled t-shirt with jeans—Veronica's grooming had taken a nosedive. A sour frown twisted her lips. She carried a large sealed box.

Neve's fingers twitched as she contemplated shutting the door in her ex-stepmother's face.

"Well, look how you've made out with Daddy helping you from the grave," Veronica sneered.

She bit down on her tongue, trying to keep from reaching out and throttling the bitch.

"Took his will money for you to find a place on your own, didn't it?" She glared down her nose at her. "Money that should've been mine."

Someone is bitter. Neve stayed silent, waiting to see why the woman had knocked on her door.

"Here." Veronica shoved the box at her. "Since Nathan's kicking me out of my house, I had to go through my stuff and found some of your old paperwork, birth certificate, and all."

Neve arched a brow. The stepmother she knew would've thrown it out regardless.

"Nathan's giving me an extension if I get the remnants of your things to you," she clarified. "Don't for a second think I'd give a waste like you any charity."

Makes more sense. She grabbed the box from her. Her jaw ached—she hadn't even realized she'd clenched it. Veronica always burned her nerves, sucking away any hope or happiness. Not like the woman would start turning things around any time soon. "Don't blame Uncle Nate. It's about time you did something on your own."

"You? Defending him?" Veronica's pink lips curled into a harsh smile. "Priceless."

The sinking feeling hit her stomach again, the same one when she'd first run into Uncle Nate. "Just stop."

"Please tell me you know." Those icy-blue eyes took on a cold glint. "You're not that oblivious, right?"

This subject wasn't getting breached. Nathan was one of the few she considered family that she had left.

"As oblivious as the woman who didn't realize the man she'd married was gay?" Neve snapped. "Leave me the hell alone. You've been a parasite since my dad left, spending his money and relying on mine. Let's see how you do when you've got to tough it on your own." Fighting against the woman who made her life hell strengthened her conviction.

Veronica's fists tightened, and her face paled. Grabbing a prescription bottle from her purse, she tossed it into the apartment. "Do everyone a favor and down the whole thing. Your mother wasn't sick, sweetheart. She killed herself, probably from the nightmare of dealing with you. Even your father abandoned you. Take the hint."

Neve's nerves flared as anger flooded her veins. This woman had torn her down for the last time. "Do you know what's truly sad? That you have nothing better to do with your life than ruin mine. If you want to see what's ugly, try looking in a mirror."

Veronica opened her mouth, for once, speechless. In that moment, Neve saw her for who she really was, just a sad, spoiled girl who blamed others instead of accepting responsibility in life. The lapse of vulnerability quickly turned to irritation, like she knew it would, and Veronica stormed away.

She shut the door, listening to her ex-stepmother's footsteps boom down the hallway as the woman left, hopefully for good. Neve blinked, her eyes burning. Veronica wasn't telling the truth—her stepmother couldn't know. Her mom had died from a heart attack. Dad would've told her.

Her fingers numbed, and she dropped the box to the floor. She sank to her knees. *Would* he have told her? He had abandoned her and retreated into his own business after Mom died. One person would know the truth, though.

Digging her phone from her purse, she made a call.

***

Neve was so uncomfortable she could scratch her own skin off. The Applebee's waitress had stopped by no less than six times, even after she explained she was waiting on someone. A place like this wasn't the best to meet, but the last thing she wanted to do was get together at the diner and have this conversation in front of the other guys.

Her upside-down reflection in the spoon stared back at her, but even with the distortion, the worry lines on her forehead gave her feelings away. She tucked the utensil under her napkin.

Uncle Nate appeared just inside the door, looking sharp in a fitted sweater, trim gray slacks, and a stylish slate military jacket. His waves were tamed and framed his long chin, testament to his silver-fox status. He waved once he saw her, lifting his sunglasses as he walked to the table.

"Nevie, is everything okay? You sounded shaken up on the phone." The slight wrinkles on his face deepened with concern.

Her fingers tapped a beat on the plastic menu. How to broach this? Did she even want the answer? Yet as she watched Uncle Nate, she knew this question wasn't one she could bury. Because, out of anyone in her family, her mother was the only one who hadn't betrayed her.

"My mom," Neve started.

He froze—only for a second, but she had caught it before he relaxed his shoulders. Her chest tightened. She was terrified to continue, afraid of what he knew. She lifted her chin. She had to find out.

"Did my mom commit suicide?" she asked, her voice near a whisper.

"Who told you that?" His voice sharpened, and his brows knitted together. Not the response she wanted.

"Doesn't matter. I need you to answer my question." She remained firm. This wasn't something they could avoid, no matter how much she wanted to.

Her heart pounded in her ears.

His lips formed a thin line. His silence gave an answer on its own.

"Why?" *Not Mom*. Not the one person who cared—she wouldn't commit suicide and leave her. Tendrils of ice seeped through her veins. *Unless Veronica is right. Unless I'm too terrible, and Mom offed herself to get away from me.*

Uncle Nate's dark eyes were glassy. His bottom lip trembled the slightest bit. Guilt poured off him in droves. He kept wiping his palms on his pants, and when she tried to look him in the eyes, he glanced away.

"She caught us, Nevie. She couldn't take the thought of her husband being—" He clapped a hand over his mouth. His eyes watered, but he refused to look at her.

Her throat tightened. She couldn't breathe. The room grew blurry until a voice snapped her to awareness.

"Can I take your order?" The waitress had returned, staring at her while tapping a pen on her pad.

Neve opened her mouth then shut it again. She swallowed a couple gulps of air, unable to focus on anything for long.

Uncle Nate scrutinized the menu, holding it like a shield.

The waitress glanced between them. "I'll get you some more water."

I'm drowning. She gasped as her gaze drifted to the other diners. To the cheesy neon lighting hanging near the door. To the gaudy, banana-yellow and flamingo-pink pictures on the wall.

"Sorry. Sorry. Sorry. Neve, I'm so sorry." Uncle Nate repeated the words over and over. Tears flowed.

Neve's feelings, however, had iced over. Even though Stephen Wynn had abandoned her, she'd always thought he'd loved her mother. She'd held onto the image of a better time, a time before her mother had died and her father had gone downhill. Turned out, he'd been sliding down his slope for far longer. With Uncle Nate.

A case of the shakes overtook her. Her fingers trembled in front of her, causing something in her brain to signal sitting here across from him wasn't going to be good for her.

"I've got to go," she mumbled, clutching her bag as she stumbled out of the booth.

Before he could say anything or try to stop her, she ducked out of the Applebee's and into the warm night. The faint breezes lifted the hairs on her arms, but not even that chill could pierce through the numbness inside. She kept to the sidewalks, focusing on the cracks. One step and another step. Focusing on that kept her moving.

"Hey stranger," a familiar voice called out.

Neve didn't stop. She couldn't. She clenched and unclenched her fingers, over and over and over.

Someone grabbed her arm. She spun around to face a tall guy in a green hoodie with those storm-blue eyes that had first caught her gaze. Feet away, the soft lights of The Cottage Diner glowed, illuminating the huge panel windows.

"What the hell?" His grip tightened. "First, I don't see or hear from you since you left, and now you're ignoring me?"

She blinked, hard. They didn't want her there, not the girl with the never-ending parade of problems.

Not when her own mother couldn't stick it out to stay by her side. Her lower lip trembled.

Brendan's eyebrows lifted in concern. "Neve, did something happen? You look like you're getting sick."

She glanced down at her arms. A thin sheen of sweat covered her pale skin. He couldn't get involved in this. She wouldn't drag anyone else down in her miserable existence, not when everyone around her ended up dead or gone. No more.

"I-I need to get home." The words came out slurred. What was wrong with her?

His hands moved to her shoulders, holding her upright. "Something's not right with you, and you're not getting out of this so fast."

"Leave me the hell alone," she snapped. She needed to get home. Had to get home. People got hurt when she was around. "I'm not some damsel in distress. I don't need your help."

Releasing her, he stepped away as if she'd slapped him. Jaw tense, he shoved his hands into his pockets, squaring those shoulders. "It's your funeral."

Her eyes stung, but she turned away from him. This is how it had to be—why didn't he understand?

She continued toward her apartment, one step at a time. Her father had been the worst, Uncle Nate was a traitor, and even her own mother left her behind when she took her life. Brendan's concern would disappear the moment some other girl danced his way. She could not handle being abandoned again. Not in the slightest.

She climbed the stairs to her apartment, the shadows widening along the corridor. As she walked into her empty place, though, none of the comfort she'd been hoping for awaited her. Instead, the dim lights cast around the room, the darkness, in its shades of gray and black, competing for loneliness. The floorboards were slick under her feet, and, as she pressed her back against the wall, the cold plaster seeped into her spine.

She'd done it this time with pushing Brendan away. Opening the can of worms with Uncle Nate. She threw her bag against the wall, and her keys came tumbling out, hitting the small bottle of pills she'd never thrown in the trash.

Do everyone a favor and take the whole bottle.

Veronica's poisonous words echoed in her mind.

It's your funeral.

Brendan had given up, like she knew he would, like everyone did. Even her own mother had abandoned her, preferring death to spending life with her daughter. Uncle Nate's sobs filled her head along with a never-ending chorus of *sorry* sinking the dagger a little deeper with each round. She banged her head against the wall and stared at the ceiling. Her bones ached with weariness, and her chest tightened, making it difficult to breathe.

Take the hint.

Neve reached over and grabbed the bottle, shaking out the pills, small red circular ones littering her hand like sores. Her hand wouldn't move though. Such a simple motion, but she couldn't bring them to her lips. She glanced outside at the sky, filled with clouds and smog. All the pollution, all that hell—even the stars didn't stand a chance.

Her stepmother had done enough damage to her life. Ever since her father had left, she'd allowed the woman to be around, to influence her. No more. The pills fell from her hands as she stood, making her way to the small, empty kitchen she had.

She unscrewed the cap on the bottle of Wild Turkey that Uncle Nate got her for a housewarming gift. Revelations were something she couldn't handle right now. Numb—she needed to be numb. Mom had been a coward, just like Dad. Both of them had fucked off and abandoned her.

The pinch in her chest grew painful and her eyes burned. Each breath she took was shakier than the last, but every time she tried to grasp onto a coherent thought, it spun out of control. She poured herself a glass of bourbon, focusing on the amber liquid as it swirled around the cup.

The first swallow caused her to splutter, but she persevered.

As the liquid warmed her chest, the first tears began to fall, coursing down her cheeks. She gasped, choking on her sobs as she tried to hold them back. No such luck. She slumped against the back of her cabinets, sitting on the tiled floor of her kitchen. Her shoulders shook, and her hands trembled. Yet the glass in her hand whispered promises of relief.

This was her reset. The new apartment, a new life away from Veronica, but her past hounded her wherever she ran. She took another gulp from the glass—the liquid no longer burned going down, only filled her chest with the warmth she'd had missing for a long time.

Her father had caused it all—the man who never should've been a father. Her mother had run away. Neve's mind skipped on that. The thought contradicted every memory she had of the woman, of the times at the park, or the way her mother sang while she cooked. Her mother had been bright, sunny, and the one good thing in her life.

Yet, she'd abandoned her, just like Dad. Her cheeks heated with the same fury in her chest.

The room blurred around the edges. Every sip numbed her a little more, until finally, the tears stopped, their damp tracks drying on her face. She refilled her cup.

The glass almost slipped from her hands as she fumbled with it. A deep breath shuddered through her as she slumped forward, entranced by the shifting liquid in her glass. The glow of the bulb penetrated through the amber, but even as she drank, it never reached her. Tonight was the bleak sort of night that banished any memory of the sun's warmth. Tonight was another night of fighting to survive the hell she'd been through.

But alone like this, without a single person to turn to, tonight, she needed a little help.

Her eyelids kept slipping shut, even as she tried to keep them open, and her heartbeat echoed in her ears. Maybe, just for a moment, she could let go.

Chapter Thirteen

B lack. Everything around her was black.

Neve tried opening her eyes, but they refused to budge. Her arms wouldn't move, nor her legs, as if duct tape bound her entire body tight. Everything hurt, from her forearms to her toes, like she'd been battered with hammers and thrown in a ditch. Her breaths were even though, cyclical.

The last thing she remembered was sitting in her kitchen with a glass of bourbon. *So, why can't I open my* eyes? She'd never had a hangover like this before.

Veronica, Uncle Nate, Brendan...everything urgent faded into the background of her mind. The truth about her mother—it hurt like a dull throb, like her body ached but not with the intensity of the other night. Not the stinging burn of a knife dragged over an open wound.

Faint murmurs sounded around her, but she couldn't see and couldn't move.

Something warm pressed against her lips. The motion was soft and gentle. Her body responded—pins and needles coursed into her arms, overwhelming warmth flooded through her, heating her cheeks. Her tender lips tingled. *This...must be heaven. What it feels like to be loved.*

Tears burned her eyes, coursed down her cheeks. Her eyelashes fluttered, working once more. She blinked, blinded by the sharp white light in the room.

Neve sighed. She'd regained a little more control. White walls and fluorescent lights. The rest of the room blurred. She blinked, trying to get the residue out of her eyes since her hand's response was delayed.

That smell. Stale bleach and death. She was in a hospital.

Her vision returned at last. An IV patched onto her arm, delivering to her best guess, a saline solution. The sheets were a faded seafoam green, adding to the fluorescent glare of the room. Machines dangled all around her, and the dull click, click of a monitor thrummed through the room.

"Neve." The voice was filled with hoarse concern, something she'd never heard from him before.

With effort, she turned her head. Brendan stood next to her bed, clutching the rail. His knuckles were white and his eyebrows furrowed together. The second their eyes met, a shudder ran through her so fierce tears welled.

"Were you trying to drink yourself to death?" Despite the anger in his voice, his face was pale, his eyes red rimmed.

She scratched behind her ear, still confused. "What happened?"

This sort of vulnerable concern wasn't what she'd expected from him. She remembered tossing the pills out and having a drink to numb the pain. Except it had been a bit more than one drink. *Shit*.

"Before I went home, I decided to check on you since you'd seemed off earlier. When I stepped into your apartment, that's when I found you."

Her cheeks heated with shame. She'd hit a

desperate low, and if he hadn't followed her, they might not be having this conversation.

"I'm not going to ask what caused you to hit the bottle last night. From what I've seen, you've had a hellish life, and I'm sure I haven't been much help." He shoved his hands into his pockets as he stared down at the floor. "All I know is that I've missed you, and last night made me realize a couple things."

She curled her fingers into the sheets, not knowing what to expect. Not that she'd ever expected to wake up with Brendan at her side. "It made me realize I need to get a restraining order for a certain ex-family member," she mumbled.

That brought a twist of a smile from him. He took in a deep breath, "From day one, it's like you've burrowed into my mind. You're all I think about. The one person I want to be around. You might've thought it was charity, but having you in my apartment? For once I didn't feel lonely. Not like you'd know with the way I acted." He grimaced. "But I was getting over Stacy." He shook his head then lifted his gaze to hers. "The thought of us together terrified me. I thought I'd finally found someone who

I didn't have to pretend around. I was afraid I'd ruin it. That I'd lose you."

Funny thing about numbing the pain—after drinking herself stupid last night, all she wanted was to feel. This rush of warmth, the elation it sent through her mind, was everything she'd wanted, everything that all the loss and grief had made her forget. At last, she didn't have to throw up her shields or hide behind her defenses because Brendan felt the same way she did. Her heart raced, like it always did when he was near, but the fear didn't follow that he would abandon her like everyone else. Because he'd done the opposite—he had returned, even after she pushed him away.

"It's about time." Her voice came out soft.

He stopped scuffing the floor and looked at her, like he saw straight through her. All her pent-up emotion—everything she'd been holding inside flooded out. He had eyes like a storm at sea, but she was ready to dive into the depths.

Reaching out, he lifted her chin with his fingers. Locked in on his gaze, she couldn't look away. She could almost taste those lips on hers. The scent of his pine aftershave lingered in the air around them, sending the same thrill through her that raced to her fingertips. His breath mingled with hers but this time, no whisky. Her surroundings melted away, a blur compared to the heat blazing inside her chest and the fire in his eyes. For a single moment, no one else existed—just the two of them.

Brendan leaned in, pressing his lips against hers. The second they kissed, she knew.

He was the one who had brought her back to life.

About the Author

Katherine McIntyre is an author of steampunk adventure, dark comedy, urban fantasy and paranormal romance stories. She splits her time writing and working the day job, but as for creative pursuits, she's dabbled in a little bit of everything. A modern day Renaissance-woman, she's learned soapmaking, beer brewing, tea blending and most recently roasting coffee. The one constant from a very young age was her passion for reading and writing.

You may visit with Katherine at:
http://katherine-mcintyre.com

Other Books by Katherine

Soul Solution

By the Sea